"Do you know," Rafe said, "just how lovely you are?"

He pulled Maggie's hat from her head, then toyed with one of her ponytails. "The sun turns your hair to golden honey and makes your eyes sparkle. And you have such a beautiful smile. You rarely smile at me, lass—do you know that?"

She wanted to escape him, at least she thought she did. But her legs refused to obey her, and her hands clung to his shoulders with no will of her own. "I . . . I thought we were going to look at the horses," she murmured.

"Horses." His smile grew crooked, and his eyes filled with something like regret. "Sometimes I've wished I were a horse, Maggie. I'd have all your attention then. I'd feel your hands stroking me, hear your soft voice praising me. And you'd look at me with a smile in your eyes." His laugh was self-mocking. "That's how I feel. I want all your time, all your attention. I want to hold you. Kiss you." His arms tightened around her, and his lips grazed hers. "I want to see you look at me with desire, feel your hands touching my skin. Is it so wrong to want that?"

She couldn't answer, couldn't find the words or the breath for them. And when his head lowered and blotted out the sun, she couldn't find the strength to turn her head aside. . . .

WHAT ARE *LOVESWEPT* ROMANCES?

They are stories of true romance and touching emotion. We believe those two very important ingredients are constants in our highly sensual and very believable stories in the *LOVESWEPT* line. Our goal is to give you, the reader, stories of consistently high quality that may sometimes make you laugh, sometimes make you cry, but are always fresh and creative and contain many delightful surprises within their pages.

Most romance fans read an enormous number of books. Those they truly love, they keep. Others may be traded with friends and soon forgotten. We hope that each *LOVESWEPT* romance will be a treasure—a "keeper." We will always try to publish

LOVE STORIES YOU'LL NEVER FORGET
BY AUTHORS YOU'LL ALWAYS REMEMBER

The Editors

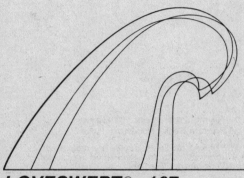

LOVESWEPT® • 167

Kay Hooper
The Shamrock Trinity:
Rafe, The Maverick

 BANTAM BOOKS
TORONTO • NEW YORK • LONDON • SYDNEY • AUCKLAND

THE SHAMROCK TRINITY: RAFE, THE MAVERICK

A Bantam Book / November 1986

*LOVESWEPT® and the wave device are registered
trademarks of Bantam Books, Inc. Registered in U.S. Patent
and Trademark Office and elsewhere.*

Cover art by Joe Devito.

ISBN 0-553-21786-0

Published simultaneously in the United States and Canada

*Bantam Books are published by Bantam Books, Inc. Its
trademark, consisting of the words "Bantam Books" and
the portrayal of a rooster, is Registered in U.S. Patent and
Trademark Office and in other countries. Marca Registrada.
Bantam Books, Inc., 666 Fifth Avenue, New York, New
York 10103.*

PRINTED IN THE UNITED STATES OF AMERICA

O   0 9 8 7 6 5 4 3 2 1

Some things, like Topsy, just grow. A thought becomes a suggestion . . . an idea . . . a plot. "What if . . . ?" becomes "Well, maybe . . ." and finally "That might work!"

For the endless hours of work, the conference calls, the batting back-and-forth of ideas, the patience, good humor, generosity, and utter professionalism, I'd like to dedicate this book to my co-conspirators in a truly dastardly plot:
Iris Johansen and Fayrene Preston

Preface

It was said that the Delaneys were descended from Irish kings and were still kissing cousins to half of Europe's royalty. Being more than an ocean away, Europe's royalty could scarcely confirm this.

Luckily for the Delaneys.

Old Shamus Delaney was wont to speak reminiscently of various cattle reivers, cutthroats, and smugglers in his family, but only when good Irish whiskey could pry such truths out of him. Sober, he held to it tooth and nail that the Delaneys were an aristocratic family—and woe to any man who dared dispute him.

They were a handsome family: tall and strong of body, quick and keen of mind. Nearly all of them had dark hair, but their eyes varied from Kelly-green to sky-blue, and it seemed at least one person of every generation boasted black eyes that could flash with Delaney temper or smile with Delaney charm.

None could deny that charm. And none could deny that the Delaneys carved their empire with their own hands and wits. Royalty they may not have been, but if Arizona had been a country, the Delaneys would have been kings.

Whatever his bloodlines, Shamus Delaney sired strong sons, who in turn passed along the traits suitable to building an empire. Land was held in the teeth of opposition, and more was acquired until the empire spread over five states. Various businesses were tried; some abandoned and some maintained. Whenever there was a call to battle, the Delaney men took up arms and went to war.

Many never came home.

In the first generations, an Apache maiden caught a roving Delaney eye, and so the blood of another proud race enriched Delaney stock. Sometime before the turn of this century a Delaney daughter fell in love with a Spanish don who really could claim a royal heritage. She was widowed young, but her daughter married a Delaney cousin, so there was royal blood of a sort to boast of.

They were a canny lot, and clan loyalty was strong enough to weather the occasional dissensions that could tear other great families apart. The tides in their fortune rose and fell, but the Delaney luck never entirely deserted them. They built a true dynasty in their adopted land, and took for their symbol the shamrock.

They were a healthy family, a lucky family, but not invulnerable. War and sickness and accidents took their toll, reducing their number inexorably. Finally there was only a single Delaney son controlling the vast empire his ancestors had built. He, too, answered the call to battle in a world war, and when it was over, he answered another call—this one from the land of his ancestors. He was proud to find the Delaney name still known and respected, and fierce in his newfound love for the land of his family's earliest roots.

But his own roots were deeply set in the soil of Arizona, and at last he came home. He brought with him a bride, a true Irish colleen with merry black eyes and a soft, gentle touch. And he promised her and himself that the Delaney family would grow again.

While his country adjusted to a life without war, and prosperity grew, Patrick Delaney and his wife, Erin, set about building their family. They had three sons: Burke, York, and Rafe.

As the boys grew, so did the empire. Patrick was a canny businessman, expanding what his ancestors had built until the Delaney family employed thousands. Ventures into mining and high finance proved lucrative, and the old homestead, Killara, expanded dramatically.

By the time twenty-one-year-old Burke was in college, the Delaney interests were vast and complex. Burke was preparing to assume some of the burden of the family business, while nineteen-year-old York was graduating from high school, and seventeen-year-old Rafe was spending every spare moment on a horse, any horse, at the old Shamrock Ranch.

Then tragedy struck. On their way to Ireland for a long-overdue vacation, Patrick and Erin Delaney were killed in a plane crash, leaving three sons to mourn them.

Leaving three sons . . . and a dynasty.

One

"Dammit, Tom! Grab his head!" Rafe Delaney picked himself up from the dirt for the third time and scowled through the kicked-up dust of the corral at the plunging, squealing black stallion they'd named Diablo . . . for a reason.

Tom Graham managed to tie the stallion to the post in the center of the corral, swiftly moving his lanky frame when Diablo lashed out viciously with both forelegs. Limping a bit from an earlier kick, Tom crossed the corral to stand beside his boss. "Let 'im settle down some," he suggested. "And us too. Been a long time since we've had to saddle-break a real wild one."

Brushing off his jeans, Rafe agreed with a nod. It *had* been a long time. Training horses to accept riders was accomplished by much calmer and gentler methods these days. Unless a renegade like Diablo came along. For weeks now he'd thrown

Rafe at least twice a day. When he couldn't dislodge his rider any other way, he simply threw himself over backward—a dangerous and deadly habit in a horse.

Rafe was near the point of admitting defeat, something he'd never done before. Only the Thoroughbred's worth as a stud had convinced Rafe to buy the horse that no one had been able to handle in six years of trying. But if Diablo couldn't be handled, he was certainly too dangerous to breed. Heaven only knew what insane traits he'd pass on to offspring.

"May I try?"

Rafe swung around to see a kid sitting on the top rail of the fence. If she stood five feet tall, he thought fleetingly, it would only be because of the heels on her English-style, knee-high boots. Jeans molded her slender legs and hips, and a white cotton blouse showed tanned forearms and throat. Her long blond hair was caught in ponytails beneath each ear, and her face was shadowed by a billed cap. There was something vaguely familiar about her, but he couldn't be sure what it was.

"I don't know who you are, kid," Rafe said impatiently, "but I don't make it a habit to watch cheerful suicides! If you're looking for someone—"

"I am." She dropped lightly to the ground inside the corral and approached him, looking even smaller than he'd imagined her to be. She halted before him and met his stare, her own violet eyes amused but slightly wary. "I'm looking for you, Mr. Delaney. I'm Maggie O'Riley—and if the thirty-day trial works out, I'm your new trainer."

Rafe heard Tom choke in astonishment, but his own attention was entirely focused on the woman standing before him. And, at twenty-six years of age, she *was* a woman. He remembered all the information in her letter of application. And all the glowing recommendations regarding her ability with horses. And he remembered . . . "You looked much bigger on that hunter at Madison Square Garden, Miss O'Riley."

She smiled just a little. "He wasn't as big as he looked," she said. "Made me look bigger."

"You're still too damn small," he said with the frankness that had gotten him into trouble more than once.

It got him into trouble again.

Slender shoulders squared and violet eyes glared into his with no softness at all. "I'd heard that Shamrock was an open-minded, *progressive* ranch, Mr. Delaney. I hadn't expected to be condemned for lack of inches. Just for the record, I've handled horses all my life, from training ring to show ring, and I've never yet been thrown twice by the same horse. Not, I may add, because I didn't get back on." She glanced pointedly at the dust on Rafe's jeans.

"Now, look . . ." he began in the modified lion's roar that would have warned anyone who knew him to hide until the storm passed.

"No, *you* look!" she snapped, staring up at him fiercely. "I was promised thirty days trial, and that's what I'll get. I won't be refused before getting a chance to prove myself. And I'll start," she finished with a nod toward Diablo, "with *that* horse."

"The hell you will! The best horsemen in the Southwest have tried that horse for six years—and you think *you* can break him? You couldn't hold his head up, and he'd toss you like a rag doll on the first jump!"

"Are you a betting man, Mr. Delaney?" she asked icily.

He glared at her.

She glanced up at the blazing midday sun, ignoring his silence. "I'll ride that horse by sunset—or I'll leave, and you can find yourself a nice, *big* trainer for your horses."

"You're on," he said instantly.

Maggie O'Riley nodded calmly. "Fine. Do you mind getting the saddle off him, please?"

"Why?" he asked suspiciously.

"Because I won't handle a horse someone else has saddled. And I'll need a dandy brush and some water."

Rafe's black brows rose, but he merely gestured toward the nearest of the many long barns. "Tackroom's to the left of the hall. Help yourself."

By the time Maggie returned with the brush and a pail of water, Rafe and his foreman had managed to get Diablo unsaddled, though not without a good deal of sweating and swearing. The big horse stood tied to the post in the center of the corral, lathered and enraged. As Maggie leaned over the top rail to set the pail inside, then climbed easily over the fence, Diablo was furiously trying to tear his hitching post out of the ground.

"He's all yours," Rafe told her sardonically.

"What's his name?"

"Diablo—and he earned it."

She glanced at Rafe coolly, then picked up the pail and headed for the big horse. As she drew closer to the animal, it seemed to Rafe she looked smaller and smaller. The contrast between more than half a ton of devil-horse and a hundred pounds or so of woman was ridiculous, and Rafe began to have second thoughts.

"Tom, get ready in case he charges," he said quickly. "That damn horse'll kill her." Both he and the older man braced themselves to race forward and save the tiny woman from certain mauling, if not death.

However . . .

She set the pail down out of reach of the stallion, then approached him slowly and steadily. Diablo screamed and lashed out with his forelegs, but she never hesitated. Halting just a couple of feet from him, she stood motionless. The stallion began to quiet, his white-rimmed eyes still wildly suspicious and his ears flicking nervously, and the two tensely waiting men caught the woman's faint, wordless crooning. They exchanged puzzled glances, then turned their attention back to the center of the corral.

Maggie remained exactly where she was for nearly half an hour, her patience incredible. She stepped closer to the horse only when he was finally still, then walked steadily to his head. Diablo made a clearly halfhearted attempt to bite her, which she evaded easily. Using the dandy brush, she began gently stroking the horse's wet neck and shoulders, still crooning wordlessly.

She brushed him from neck to rump before getting the pail and allowing the horse a few mouthfuls of water. The ritual was repeated twice more, by which time Diablo was standing perfectly quiet, his eyes no longer white-rimmed. Then she untied the stallion and led him at a calm walk around the corral while he cooled and the sweat dried on his gleaming body.

The two silently watching men were more relaxed now, though both were nonetheless ready for instant action. They were all too aware that any stallion could be one of the most dangerous, unpredictable animals on earth. Especially this one.

But as they waited throughout the long, hot afternoon, it became clear that Diablo—for whatever inscrutable equine reason—had decided to bend his proud neck to a mistress rather than a master. Before the men's astonished eyes the stallion even nudged her affectionately as she was strapping the hated saddle on his back.

And when the sun was still a good hour above the horizon, Maggie swung lightly into the saddle and loped the big horse sedately around the corral. Diablo pinned his ears back each time he passed the men, but was otherwise a model of calm obedience.

"Boss," Tom said slowly, "didn't you hire her to handle those new gaited horses you bought?"

Too much a horseman to feel jealousy at Maggie's skill, Rafe was watching her with admiration. "Yeah," he said. "I saw her ride hunters and gaited horses in New York, and when I asked around for a trainer, she was recommended. She's a top money-winner on the East Coast, and she's ridden for every major stable you could name. According to her letter, she'd decided to leave the circuit and take a permanent job as trainer." Rafe grinned suddenly at his foreman. "And I think we got a bargain, Tom."

Tom grinned in response, his faded blue eyes twinkling. "You'll have to eat crow, boss."

"Don't I know it! Well, she proved me wrong. If she can handle that hellion, she can handle any other horse we've got. She's earned the right to gloat."

But Maggie didn't gloat. Dismounting from

Diablo, she merely said, "I'd like to stable him myself."

"This way," Rafe said. Tom swung the gate open, and Rafe led the way to Diablo's stable. He watched silently as she unsaddled and groomed the stallion. She still looked incredibly small and delicate next to the big horse, but Rafe didn't have to be hit over the head to absorb a lesson: She was bigger than she looked.

"Miss O'Riley," he said formally as soon as Diablo was contentedly munching hay in his stable, "if you still want to work for a hotheaded Irishman, the job's yours—and never mind the trial period."

She faced him solemnly, making him realize her tempers were as quickly over as his own. "I'm Irish, too, Mr. Delaney, and somewhere back among my ancestors, the name O'Riley meant 'warlike.' I can take it if you can."

They shook hands gravely, then both began to laugh.

"I'm Maggie," she said.

"And I'm Rafe. No formality around here. Happy to have you aboard, Maggie."

"Happy to be here. I think," she added cautiously.

Rafe winced. "My big mouth. But you have to admit you looked like a kid sitting on that fence." When she rolled her eyes, he said, "And you've heard that before, I take it."

"Constantly." Maggie had weighed up her employer by now, taking her own impressions and comparing them to what she'd heard about Rafe Delaney and Shamrock Ranch. As they walked toward the ranch house she listened with only half an ear as he briskly described the layout of the place. She knew the layout of Shamrock because she'd done thorough research before applying for the position.

She'd also done research on Rafe Delaney. He was, quite literally, one third of a dynasty. It was said by some that the Delaney brothers didn't own all of Arizona simply because a reprobate ancestor had lost part of it in a crooked poker game shortly before the Civil War. That reprobate's smarter—and luckier—ancestors had trundled their covered wagons across virgin America, fighting indians all the way, only to fall in love with land a far cry from the Old Country.

And now, the twentieth-century descendants of all that vital blood comprised one of the last true dynasties. There were only three Delaneys now, Maggie knew. At thirty-six Burke was the oldest; he controlled the finances for the family. York, thirty-four, handled the oil and mining properties. And Rafe, thirty-two, managed Shamrock Ranch, which was known throughout the country for producing magnificent Thoroughbreds, Arabians, and Quarter horses.

All three brothers were unmarried.

Maggie glanced covertly at her new boss as they walked companionably up the wide lane to the ranch house. She'd never seen the other two Delaney brothers, but Rafe certainly showed evidence of his rakish heritage. Irish, Mexican, and Indian—heaven knew what tribes!—blood had produced in this brother a curious wild gypsy appearance. His black hair was thick and a bit shaggy, a stubborn lock falling over his forehead. Winged brows flew above eyes of gleaming ebony, eyes that had a laughing devil in them.

His nose had been broken at some point since it was now faintly crooked, and his smile . . . his smile, Maggie thought wryly, could melt an ice-berg. He had the high cheekbones and the bronze skin of his triple heritage, and the broad-shoul-dered, whipcord-lean frame of an active man who used every muscle in his work. And beautiful hands, long-fingered, strong, graceful. The kind of hands, she mused, that could handle a newborn foal with gentleness, a powerful stallion with firm-ness, and a woman with tenderness.

Instantly she pushed the last thought out of her mind.

As to personality, Maggie had heard some and deduced some. By reputation, he was a true horse-man with endless patience for the animals he handled and the people in his employ. From all reports Rafe "took care" of his people as the Delaneys had always taken care of their own.

There was clearly enough Irish blood left in him to produce a respectable tot of blarney. He had the deep, lilting voice of a born charmer, and if he hadn't broken a few hearts in the last fifteen years or so, Maggie didn't know her own sex. Her meet-ing with him had revealed a temper that was quickly over, but as dangerous as a thunderhead for the duration. She'd heard it said that Rafe could laugh off any insult to himself, but would instantly go to the mat—literally—over any slight to his brothers.

But once the fight was over, he tended to help bandage his enemies and buy a round of drinks to show there were no hard feelings. Hotheaded he certainly was, but Maggie had heard a great deal about his kindness and generosity. He was appar-ently the kind of man children and animals adored, other men sincerely liked, and women could love with disastrous ease.

Disastrous because in roughly ten years of cutting a bachelor swath through all points west of the Mississippi—and, according to rumor, a great deal of Europe the summer after college—Rafe's roguish fancy had been, to say the least, fickle. Maggie had heard no breath of scandal, but it seemed Rafe had successfully avoided numerous matrimonial snares and several almost compromising situations. She had no doubt he'd been charming; quite likely he'd been genuinely distressed by tearful recriminations. The fact remained, though, that the man was a potential heartache for any woman dumb enough to take him seriously.

Granted, she thought, rumor abounded where the Delaney brothers were concerned, and not all of it was kind. But she had turned her listening ears to the bluntly honest grapevine composed of people in the horse business—breeders, riders, trainers, et cetera—and was reasonably sure she had a clear perspective on Rafe Delaney. In the surprisingly tight-knit community of horsemen and women, he was respected and trusted, his judgment held as expert, and his word concerning horses considered as good as gold.

Maggie knew of three different breeders who sincerely liked Rafe, encouraged and enjoyed his infrequent visits to their farms in pursuit of more stock, and trusted him implicitly. But each man made certain his daughter was out of town whenever Rafe visited. It was not, each insisted, that he didn't trust the man. It was just that Rafe Delaney could charm the devil out of both his horns and tail—and daughters were sometimes silly. . . .

She glanced aside to see his strong, perhaps even arrogant, profile. But humor curved his mouth and shimmered in the dark eyes. There was, she thought, a raw vitality in his movements, in his very presence. He was like a Thoroughbred: bold and confident and reckless in his strength.

The realization awoke something unfamiliar within Maggie, and she shied away from probing the feeling. But she couldn't escape the sensation of restless, liquid heat stirring inside her.

Maggie reminded herself she was an employee of Shamrock Ranch and Rafe Delaney. Period. Rafe wanted to expand his operations to include gaited horses and possibly dressage, and he would hardly shell out a small fortune to his new trainer if that was a momentary interest on his part. He'd hired her to train horses, not provide a bit of light romance.

Disgusted with herself, Maggie wondered why she was even thinking about her new employer's personal life. It was none of her business, after all. She'd struggled for years to gain respect in her profession, and now finally she had been hired as trainer for one of the top three ranches in the country. It was a feather to brighten any horsewoman's cap, and she was certain to be too busy to think of romance at all.

Especially with the boss.

As they reached the top of the lane, Rafe saw Maggie's Jeep and horse trailer parked near the house, and he suddenly remembered something. "You were bringing your two horses, weren't you?" He looked down at the woman walking beside him, strongly aware of delicate features beneath the brim of her cap.

For all his easy charm Rafe tended to hold himself a bit aloof when meeting someone for the first time. He was surprised to realize how attracted he was to this woman. It wasn't her beauty, he thought, but the strength and wariness in her eyes that intrigued him. That, and the graceful way she moved. As he stared at her, he almost forgot his own question. There was something about her direct violet eyes that had a curious effect on his breathing.

She nodded. "One of your men showed me where I could stable my horses before I went looking for you." As they passed the trailer she added, "They're young. Calypso, my mare, is a Tennessee Walking Horse and Dust Devil, my stallion, is an American Saddlebred. Both of them are five-gaited."

"Champions?" he asked, a gleam in his eyes.

Reading the gleam accurately, Maggie smiled. "Champions. And excellent bloodlines. If your experiment works out and you decide to start breeding—"

"You'll work out something with me and let yours stand at stud?" he finished hopefully.

Very conscious of the charm in Rafe's grin, Maggie reminded herself yet again that this man was her boss. "I imagine we could work out something if you wanted to," she said mildly.

"Great!" Rafe paused at the neat walkway leading to a sprawling Spanish stucco ranch house, a peculiar hesitancy in his expression as he gazed toward the front door. Then he sighed and led the way up the walk. "I don't know about you, but I'm starved. We can talk about what I'm hoping to accomplish with this new venture over dinner, all right?"

"Fine."

He hesitated yet again on the tiled porch, looking down at her a bit uncertainly. "There's . . . just one thing I should mention."

"What?" she asked warily.

"Well, it's not an intent to ravish, so you can stop looking like that," he said, his eyes filled with laughter.

Maggie could feel herself flushing wildly, which was a hell of a note, because she wasn't a blushing kind of woman. "What," she said evenly, "did you want to mention?"

His smile may have been trying to hide but, if so, it was failing. "As I'm sure you recall, part of your salary is the use of a house in which to live. All my cottages are full except for one nobody's lived in for years. It'll be a nice place when the army of workmen I threw into it gets finished, but that may be a week or more. We're so far away from *anything* that it'd be ridiculous for you to stay anywhere but here at the ranch. So," he finished plaintively, "if I provide a lock for your bedroom door, would you mind staying here in the main house until yours is ready? I *have* a housekeeper for propriety's sake."

"Very funny," she managed, feeling herself flush again, but fighting a giggle at his solemn face and laughing eyes.

"You've been listening to gossip," he accused, feigning pain. "I only ravish maidens when the moon's full, so if you hear me baying, bolt your door." He sighed. "Condemned and hanged without even a trial."

"I *said* I was sorry."

"You did no such thing."

"Take it as read," she murmured.

Rafe appeared to consider the matter. "Just this once, then, but next time I'll demand a full-scale apology. Simply because gossips insist I've a tail secreted in one pant leg—"

"All right!"

Deadpan, Rafe swung open one of the big, heavy double doors. "Come into my parlor . . ."

Mentally berating herself both for listening to gossip and for letting this smooth-talking Irishman charm her, Maggie swept regally past him into the house—and stopped dead.

From the foyer she could see several rooms: a den, what looked like a library, and a formal dining room. A hallway led off to the right to what was most likely the bedroom wing of the large house. But it wasn't the layout of rooms that held Maggie's startled attention, it was the incredible clutter. There was nothing *dirty* about the house, but the profusion of things that should have been put away was amazing.

A tall stack of newspapers graced the foyer table, the bottom layers yellowed by passing time. Riding whips and spurs, along with at least three separate pairs of Western boots, were visible in the den, and magazines had overflowed the coffee table to fall haphazardly onto the floor. Books were scattered here and there, as were pillows rightly belonging on the couch. It was a mess.

Instinct told Maggie that Rafe was not that sloppy and, besides, he'd said he had help. "I thought you said you have a housekeeper."

He sighed. "For my sins, I do."

She looked up to see that peculiar hesitancy in his eyes again. "An old girlfriend getting even?" she asked dryly, then winced inwardly. *Why* couldn't she get off that particular subject? But Rafe was laughing.

"If it were only that! Unfortunately my problem is a bit more complicated. Obviously I have the world's worst housekeeper."

"Ever thought of getting another?" Maggie suggested politely.

"Dammit, I can't." Raking one hand through his thick hair, he looked down at her dolefully. "Kathleen's been with the family longer than I have. After our parents were killed, she started keeping house for my oldest brother. Burke put up with her until he couldn't take it anymore, then passed her on to York. When York couldn't take her anymore, he passed her on to me. But I didn't have anybody to pass her on to, so now I'm stuck with her."

Maggie choked on a laugh.

"I try to keep things neat myself," he went on, "but with so much work to do outside . . . Kathleen can't cook very well, although she hasn't poisoned me yet. I average losing at least one shirt a week in the laundry. Heaven knows how, exactly, and *she* certainly doesn't. And the hell of it is"—he stared around him, bewildered—"she cleans. I mean, I've seen her do it. She dusts and polishes and mops and vacuums, but somehow it never *looks* as if she does."

"I don't suppose," Maggie said unsteadily, "she'd consider retiring?"

"Fifteen years until she's sixty-five," Rafe said despairingly, "but she'll never retire. She's looking forward to 'doing for your sons, Mr. Rafe.' If only I had a third cousin to send her to . . ."

Maggie leaned against the archway leading off to the right and laughed herself silly. By the time she straightened and wiped her streaming eyes, Rafe had gone outside to the Jeep and returned with her two bags.

"This can't be all your worldly possessions," he said, hefting the bags.

"No," she agreed, "but I was thinking of the thirty-day trial. Most of my things are in storage with friends. When the house is ready, I'll send for them." It occurred to Maggie as she followed him to the bedroom wing that Rafe Delaney had quite effortlessly charmed her into his house. She decided to think about that later.

He led her past half a dozen bedrooms, then deposited her bags just inside the door of the room at the end of the hall. It was a light, airy bedroom—sitting room with sliding glass doors opening out onto the veranda at the back of the house. A large bathroom was to the left, and double closets to the right. Decorated in restful shades of blue and green, it was surprisingly neat, and Maggie couldn't help but look at Rafe questioningly.

Leaning against the doorjamb, he grinned disarmingly. "Yesterday was Kath's day off, and I hired my foreman's sixteen-year-old daughter to get this room ready for you."

Maggie didn't ask why he hadn't made a similar arrangement for the remainder of the house. She knew why. It would have hurt Kathleen's feelings, and he couldn't bring himself to do that.

She smiled. "If you don't mind, I'm going to take a shower and change before dinner."

Rafe nodded agreeably, straightening away from the jamb. "I'm going to do the same. Then," he added dryly, "I'll see what Kath's taken out of the freezer for our so-called meal. Just come out whenever you're ready." He closed the door behind him as he left.

Maggie stared at the closed door for a long moment, lost in thought. *Was* she being unfair to Rafe by accepting his reputation as truth? He had surprised and disconcerted her with his instant

perception and casual references to that reputation. The question was, Had he played truth for
laughs, or had he played false gossip for laughs?

Was Rafe Delaney a reckless heartbreaker, or
simply an attractive man whose wealth and charm
had made him notorious?

As she unpacked, Maggie reminded herself yet
again that his romantic reputation had nothing to
do with her. How weak, how uncomfortably weak
that was beginning to seem to her. Dammit, she
thought, the man *was* attractive, and she was having a difficult time keeping him in the neat mental
pigeonhole labeled BOSS.

Methodically, she finished unpacking, then took
a quick shower. After dressing in fresh clothing
she braided her long hair into a single neat plait
and tried to define her reaction to Rafe.

The first impression had been of a strong-willed,
temperamental man, his face a bit too unconventional for good looks. The devil brows above black
eyes had been too sardonic for handsomeness, his
unsmiling mouth too grim. But then he had
smiled. The deep voice had been amused, the eyes
willingly acknowledging he'd been at fault, and
Maggie had felt her heart flutter. He had looked at
her with respect and admiration, charm, making
his unconventional features exude warmth and
sincerity.

Maggie gazed unseeingly at her reflection in the
bathroom mirror. What would Rafe's personal
magnetism do to her plans? She had decided a
year ago to quit the gypsy life-style of following the
show circuit; she was more than ready for a home.
She'd spent the better part of the past ten years on
the move. Eventually she wanted to own a ranch or

stud farm, and had begun planning carefully for that years ago.

The invitation to work for Shamrock fit perfectly into her plans, and so did Rafe's obvious delight at the prospect of having her stallion stand at stud for his mares. Shamrock didn't stint on stud fees, so she could look forward to making good money for her stallion's services. Maggie had found out that Rafe had recently purchased a very young American Saddlebred stallion and three young mares, as well as a Tennessee Walking stallion and two mares, one of them already in foal to a champion stud.

Shamrock did nothing on a small scale, and she'd heard only recently that Rafe had expressed interest in a score of young mares out of three top Kentucky farms.

Leaving the bathroom, Maggie paced her bedroom restlessly. Professionally she couldn't have been in a better position. She'd been given the job as trainer for gaited horses at one of the most prestigious horsebreeding operations in the country. If she did well—and she intended to—it could only enhance her reputation. And she would have the distinction of building Shamrock's reputation for champion gaited horses. It would be her training on display in show rings, which would in turn bring in mares from other establishments to breed with Shamrock stallions.

No, professionally she was exactly where she wanted to be.

Personally, however . . .

"Personally you're an idiot," she told herself aloud, fiercely. "Your work is enough. It's always been enough."

Maggie was hardly a starry-eyed girl dreaming of

Prince Charming. Virtually on her own since she was sixteen and determined on a demanding, competitive profession, she had learned early to fight for what she wanted. She had friends, both male and female, ranging from the wealthy owners of the horses she showed to the stablehands, who were little more than kids. There had been interested men at various times, but she'd had her gaze fixed on a distant pinnacle of professional achievement and had kept relationships on a friendly basis.

But now Maggie had a curiously hollow feeling in the pit of her stomach. She had reacted to Rafe Delaney more strongly than to any man she'd ever met, far too aware of his charming personality and drawn powerfully to him in spite of distrust. That hardly boded well for her professional goals. Whether or not she discounted his reputation, her own attraction to her boss posed a potential problem.

Absently she halted her pacing and glanced down at her neat jeans and knit top, then swore softly. What did it matter how she looked? The man was her boss and nothing more. Nothing. Feeling grim, Maggie headed for the door.

Two

The instant Maggie walked into the den, Rafe rose from a deep armchair and asked, "*Now* what've I done?"

Since the men she knew weren't in the habit of standing when she entered a room, Maggie was unwillingly impressed by his manners. She would find out eventually that all three of the Delaney men were "gentlemen" as far as their manners were concerned.

His question finally sank in, and she asked puzzledly, "What do you mean?"

"You look very fierce," he explained. "I'm just assuming I've done something to upset you."

"Of course not," she said, feeling herself flush—again, dammit!

"I'm glad," he said solemnly, clearly amused. "Here, sit down. Dinner, such as it is, will be ready in about an hour. Would you like a drink?"

"Whatever you're having," she managed to say, still a little unstrung. She sat down in an armchair across from his.

"Good Irish whiskey, of course," he said cheerfully, heading for the bar in one corner. He fixed their drinks and carried hers to her before sinking down in his chair. He, too, had showered, his black hair still damp and a bit mussed. He was in jeans, and the sleeves of his white shirt were rolled back to show strong, tanned forearms.

Maggie felt her fingers itching with the desire to tangle in his thick, silky-looking hair, and frowned at her glass irritably. Enough was enough, for Pete's sake! Why couldn't she keep Rafe in his pigeonhole, and out of thoughts that could only be termed "personal"?

"You checked out Shamrock before you came, didn't you?" he asked.

"Of course," she answered honestly, meeting his quizzical gaze.

He nodded. "And I, of course, checked you out, Maggie."

She'd expected nothing less.

Musingly, he said, "You've been showing professionally since you were sixteen—and winning. Gaited, hunt, dressage. Even a few summers in the rodeo circuit. You've been able to pick and choose your mounts for the past six years.

"You were born in Richmond, Virginia," he went on impersonally. "Your mother died when you were a young girl, and your father took you along with him while he worked at various stables and ranches. He's a name trainer of Grand Prix horses and is currently training in Europe. When you were sixteen, there was—according to various opinions I heard—a falling out between you and your father. I gather it had to do with a certain . . . competitiveness between the two of you. True?"

Maggie stared at him, but raised no objection to the personal history. She'd researched him just as thoroughly, after all. "True enough," she said evenly.

Still impersonal, his gaze holding hers, Rafe went on. "The two of you shared a home for a while after that, but you were virtually on your own. Because you and your father disagreed on your choice of career, it was somewhat difficult for you to get a job. Your father's highly respected, and no one wanted to hire his daughter when he made it more than obvious that he disapproved. Still, when he took a trip to Germany some years ago, you managed to find a stable owner who didn't particularly care about your father's opinion. You took a job in that stable, and delighted your employer by turning two Thoroughbred hunters from temperamental slugs into prizewinning jumpers. Within a year you were on your way to earning a reputation, and not even your father could hinder your advancement. You pleased your employer enough so that he gave you a secondhand horse trailer in decent shape. He mentioned you to other people, who in turn hired you to show their horses for a percentage of the winnings.

"You finished high school at night, then took college courses at night, too, since you worked every day. You doubled up on most of your courses, because you often had to show at night. By the time you were twenty, you'd earned enough to buy a couple of fairly cheap young horses. You trained them, showed them successfully, and sold them at a profit. The next two horses you bought were slightly more expensive, and your profit after training and showing was larger. You began riding gaited horses and performing in dressage events, and were good enough in Grand Prix jumping to earn a place on the Olympic equestrian team. You won the gold in individual events, and the team took the gold primarily because you had the fastest clean round in the finals. And you rode your own horse."

"Lady Fair," Maggie said softly, her gaze a bit unfocused. "I had to put her down a year later."

Rafe's dark eyes showed quick sympathy, one horse lover to another, but he said nothing more about her lost horse. "I gather your father continued to disapprove, even though you'd become so successful?"

Her lips twisted in a bitter smile. "*Because* I'd become successful," she said flatly. "He didn't think I could do it. He told everyone I couldn't. And . . . he never rode for an Olympic team."

Rafe nodded, hearing not only her bitterness, but also her pain. "You left Grand Prix events for a while after that, concentrating on gaited horses. You bought and trained other horses, selling at a profit every time. Two years ago you bought your present horses as colts." He grinned suddenly. "Calypso and Dust Devil—both of them with champion bloodlines and well on their way to being champions in their own right due to your training and showing. And when you received my letter offering a thirty-day trial, you bought that Jeep out front."

It was a far more comprehensive history than Maggie had expected, and she reluctantly tipped a mental hat to his ability to ferret out information. But Rafe wasn't finished.

"I talked to a few of my friends you've ridden for

recently. I was told you're a fine rider, an excellent trainer, and a model employee. You can work with any horse, get along with all kinds of people, don't cause trouble, and if something makes you mad, you never take it out on a horse." He smiled just a little, his gaze intent. "Your conduct in the ring is impeccable, you possess a vast amount of dignity for your young years, and your judgment with horses is nothing short of uncanny. If there were any personal criticisms directed toward you by former employers, they had to do with the belief that you're a bit too serious."

The last didn't surprise Maggie, since she'd been told often that she should loosen up and enjoy herself more. It had always puzzled her to be told that. She *was* enjoying her life, she thought.

Commenting only on the information in general, she said, "If you knew all that before I came, why didn't you think I could handle Diablo?"

"I told you," he said. "You looked too damn small. I've wrestled with that hellion for weeks with no result. How did you do it?" he asked with honest interest.

"My father is a born horseman," she said slowly, the praise clearly sincere—and difficult for her to express. "He was always . . . careless with money, so he was never able to afford a place of his own and always handled other people's horses. He put me on horses before I could walk, taught me everything I know about them." She paused, brooding on the complex temperament of a man who would teach her all that he knew, and then disapprove violently when she chose to use those teachings to build a career. Then she sighed and shrugged. "He used to say 'You never *broke* a young horse, you *gentled* it.' And no matter how wild the horse, he could gentle it within a day. He talked to them, treated them with the kind firmness a parent uses with a child." She shrugged again. "And he taught me. I've never stopped to wonder why I'm successful with horses, or how I can gentle a wild one. I just do what he taught me to do."

Listening intently, Rafe heard more than she said. He heard the source of her ambition, its roots deep in the father who had always been "careless with money" and forced always to work for others. He heard the determination of a young woman painfully estranged from her father *because* of that ambition—and because of her success. And he heard the deep love of a woman with horses in her blood and her soul.

Rafe had been born, as the saying went, with a silver spoon in his mouth, his family old, wealthy, and powerful. But he knew well the hard physical work that went hand in hand with horses. And he knew that for Maggie to have weathered roughly ten years in a profession in which hard physical labor was a daily thing, she had to be much stronger and tougher than she looked. And it had been twice as hard on her, he realized, because the father who could have smoothed the way for her had instead turned his back and made his disapproval painfully obvious.

After listening to her and sorting through the facts of her life, he knew that no step in her career had been taken by chance. Maggie meant to be a success, eventually her own boss, and the seriousness her previous employers had mentioned had taken her steadily up the career ladder in spite of her father.

Which explained, he thought, her wary distrust of her new employer's reputation. She wanted no personal involvement to hinder her career, and Rafe knew well that gossip painted him a cheerful seducer. He wondered how that particular myth had gotten started. Heaven knew he'd been too busy since taking over the ranch to have time for any seducing, cheerful or otherwise.

As he studied Maggie, taking in the fine-boned, delicate face emphasized by her severe hairstyle, he realized that for the first time he was no longer accepting his reputation with equanimity.

In fact, it looked like it would be a hell of a complication.

She had won his respect by standing up to him with a challenge, and his admiration by handling Diablo. But his heart had been won in the flash of an instant, when she had laughed helplessly at his predicament with his housekeeper. Her violet eyes had gleamed with amusement, her small face had lit up with endearing warmth, and her quiet, cool voice had been husky and musical in laughter.

He'd had to step outside for more than her luggage, needing a moment or so to wrestle with the abrupt emotional jolt she'd given him.

Rafe was a normal man, not at all the rapacious charmer gossips portrayed. There had occasionally been women in his life, but the relationships had been casual on both sides, ending without regrets. He'd never been quite sure how his reputation originated, but suspected the very few golddiggers he had met and neatly sidestepped during the past years. Gossip born of frustration? Perhaps. He'd never really thought about it until now, but it seemed probable, and he could accept it without cynicism. A few ladies ambitious enough to try to catch a Delaney had sown seeds in frustration, and a reputation had grown.

And he hadn't, he thought, helped matters by remaining blithely single and dating different women. But he'd *wanted* to find the right woman and get married. That was the irony of it. He'd searched consciously and unconsciously as most men did, but no woman had jolted his heart.

Until now.

And *this* lady, he knew, would do her damnedest to keep him at arm's length because of his reputation and her own ambition.

He pulled himself from his musings to find her gazing at him curiously, and hoped no emotion had shown on his face.

If he only knew what a vain hope was it. Maggie had wondered why his black eyes had seemed so abruptly bleak and his strong jaw had tensed in determination. What was he thinking to bring an expression of resolution to his lean face? She wasn't about to ask.

The expression was fleeting, though. He smiled at her, an elusive dimple appearing to the left of his mouth. "Your father obviously taught you well. Strictly speaking, Diablo isn't one of the horses I hired you to handle, but if you wouldn't mind . . . ?"

"Glad to." She returned his smile. "Do you want him trained any particular way? To show, I mean."

"No, he's seven years old now. I bought him to breed because his bloodlines are good, but he's always been too wild. Train him any way you like. I just want him to learn to be handled without going berserk."

"Fine. I'll see what I can do."

Briskly, he said, "You'll have four Saddlebreds and three Walkers in your string to begin with. I'd like to show all of 'em next year if you think they're ready. All except one mare in foal, that is. I have my eye on some good breeding stock, but we'll need to build a reputation first in the show ring."

Maggie was nodding, his plans exactly what she'd expected.

"All your stock'll be in barn number four, along with whatever tack and equipment you'll need. I've got the basics, and you can make a list of what else you want. I've hired six hands to work under you. All have experience with horses in general, but only one knows gaited. They're *your* people, and you'll train them any way you like."

She lifted a questioning brow. "No . . . interference?"

Rafe shook his head. "None. Your barn, your stock, your people. You manage as you see fit. You'll decide who handles the stock, who assists you in training, and who eventually shows. I have maintenance men to clean the stables, but you and your people are responsible for tack and equipment." He smiled slightly. "The whole point of hiring a trainer was that I know next to nothing about gaited horses. I'll expect *you* to know, whatever comes up, and you to make decisions concerning training. I'll probably be watching pretty closely—not because I doubt your competence but because I'm interested.

"We have a permanent vet on the ranch, and three other trainers employed. They handle Quarter horses, Arabians, and Thoroughbreds. I'll introduce you tomorrow. Tom Graham—the man who was with me in the corral—is general foreman. If you have a problem and can't find me, talk to Tom. We also have a blacksmith and a few other specialists. And if we decide to tackle dressage, you'll have your pick of horses to train."

Maggie could say nothing for a moment, because it was much more than she'd dared hope for. Complete control. . . . Granted, only time would tell if Rafe's "hands-off" policy where her training was concerned would pan out, but she'd never been offered such complete authority. "I'll try not to disappoint you," she managed finally.

"You won't disappoint me," he said flatly.

She wondered how he could sound so certain. For the first time in years she questioned her own abilities. *Could* she handle the responsibilities he seemed so confident of?

Time would tell that too.

Rafe sighed. "You won't disappoint me professionally, that is. Personally is another matter."

Maggie felt the muscles of her face stiffen as she stared at him warily.

With an absurdly mournful look on *his* expressive face, Rafe sighed again. "I'm going to feel very uncomfortable if you keep looking for horns, or listening for a leer in every innocent word I say."

"Don't be ridiculous," she muttered, feeling herself flush again.

"I'm not being ridiculous, I'm being honest. I *can* be honest, you know, in spite of what people say. Even when the moon's full." Realizing that Maggie wasn't going to say a word, he went on.

"I have what I believe is a normal enthusiasm for the feminine half of humankind, but if you've been warned to expect seduction, I hope you'll put it out of your mind." He ignored her stifled protest, continuing in a calm tone, "I don't make a habit of getting romantically involved with any of the ladies here on the ranch."

Maggie was surprised, and it showed, because Rafe immediately responded.

"Yes, I employ other women. My Arabian trainer, for instance, is a woman. Also a score of assistants, quite a few riders, and a number of general stable hands. Some of them have been here for *years*," he said blandly, "and I haven't put the make on them . . . yet. Feel free to ask them."

After a moment Maggie said, "I'm . . . sorry."

"Accepted. If it'll make you feel better, you're not the first to come here expecting to have to lock your bedroom door. I have to fight my reputation just the way I'd guess that you have had to fight your size. Now I *know* you're bigger than you look. Can you accept that I'm not quite what gossips paint me? For one thing, you know what ranches are like. I'm usually too damn busy for . . . uh, romance."

He had a point, and Maggie absorbed it. She was being ridiculous, and his dry voice made her realize it. His black eyes were grave, containing no devil-laughter; his expression, serious. Fleetingly she wondered if he had to go to such pains to reassure each new female employee, then dismissed the question.

"Friends?" he asked lightly.

"Friends. And I *am* sorry, Rafe."

"Don't mention it." He grinned. "Besides, after eating one of Kath's meals, you may well wish seduction was all you had to worry about!"

Right on cue, heavy footsteps sounded and a round face peered around the doorway to the den, followed by the rest of Kathleen. She was fiftyish with a medium build and bright, merry blue eyes in an amiable face. Vivid red hair was wound around her head in a braided coronet, and she was dressed simply in a light blue housedress.

"Dinner, Mr. Rafe," she said, her voice still containing a faint Irish brogue after more than thirty years on this side of the Atlantic.

He was on his feet, gesturing toward Maggie as she, too, rose from her chair. "Kathleen, this is Maggie O'Riley, our new trainer."

The housekeeper gazed fixedly at Maggie, and Maggie's eyes widened slightly. Kathleen's round face took on an oddly eager expression and a pleased smile curved her lips. "Welcome to Shamrock, Miss Maggie," she said softly.

While Maggie was replying suitably, clearly unaware of undercurrents, Rafe shot a quick look at his housekeeper. How on earth, he wondered, had the woman guessed so quickly? And she *had* guessed, because the only other woman he'd ever heard her address with that special affectionate formality was his mother.

As they made their way into the dining room, he made a mental note to be certain Kathleen didn't ruin his chances because of a wrong word to Maggie. He'd just spent a great deal of effort in convincing her he had no rakish intentions toward her. The last thing he needed was for Maggie to find out too soon that his intentions were strictly honorable. . . .

Years of getting up before dawn to attend to horses had molded an unbreakable habit with Maggie. She found herself wide awake and restless at five the next morning. The sky was still dark, the house silent, and she was clearly the first of the household to stir.

After a fruitless attempt to go back to sleep, she tossed back the covers and rose. By the time she had tidied her room and dressed herself in jeans, a short-sleeved blouse, and boots, and had braided her hair neatly, the sky was beginning to lighten. She turned off her bedside lamp, left her room, and quietly made her way to the kitchen.

Rafe had told her firmly to consider the house hers for the duration, to come and go as she liked. She wasn't entirely certain that meant free run of Kathleen's kitchen as well, but Maggie was ready for breakfast and eager to get started with her new job. Rafe had said he would show her all around the ranch and introduce her to everyone this morning, but she had no idea what time he meant to do that.

Maggie tidied the cluttered kitchen with the automatic movements of someone to whom disarray was anathema. She grimaced slightly when she realized what she'd done, but decided that Kathleen probably wouldn't notice anyway.

She found what she needed with some difficulty and had to force herself not to rearrange both cabinets and pantry into more efficient order. Within moments she'd assembled the ingredients for an omelet and had coffee perking and fresh-squeezed orange juice standing ready on the small kitchen table.

The omelet was golden brown and the kitchen filled with enticing scents when Maggie looked up suddenly, some instinct telling her she was no longer alone.

Rafe stood in the doorway, and she had to hold back a laugh at the pensive expression on his lean face. He was gazing at the omelet the way a half-starved man would look at a feast, she thought.

"Good morning," she said politely. "I hope you don't mind—or that Kathleen won't either. I was hungry."

He cleared his throat. "Morning. No, I don't mind, and Kath certainly won't. I meant to tell you last night, but I forgot. Kath's breakfasts are so lousy that I told her ages ago not to bother. I usually just scramble a few eggs or something."

Maggie turned the fluffy omelet onto a plate and glanced at the ingredients she hadn't used. "There's more than enough for two," she offered, still trying not to laugh.

His expression brightened, then turned regretful. "I didn't hire you to cook," he said uncomfortably.

Slightly uncomfortable herself because the only man she'd ever cooked for had been her father, Maggie merely set the plate on the table, said, "The coffee's ready," and turned back to the range to prepare a second omelet.

By the time her omelet was done, Rafe had poured coffee and juice for both of them, and he held her chair for her before sitting down across from her. He had done the same thing the night before, his manners seemingly automatic, and she wondered how long she'd feel awkward about accepting gestures he took for granted. She also wondered when she would begin to relax in the presence of her new boss.

The rather slapdash meal served to them the night before had kept the atmosphere between them both casual and humorous. Maggie had struggled more than once to choke back laughter at Rafe's too expressive face as one barely edible dish succeeded another. But she had retired to her room somewhat hastily, the meal barely finished, because of an entirely different emotion.

Despite Kathleen's shortcomings Rafe was still careful not to hurt the housekeeper's feelings, and that concern had roused in Maggie a strange and inexplicable surge of tenderness. The emotion had disturbed her deeply last night, and was still disturbing her this morning. She tried to think of something light and casual to say to break the long silence between them. But her mind had gone blank, and it was Rafe who spoke first.

"You are a very good cook," he said.

"Thanks. But omelets aren't hard."

"Every one of my attempts has been," he said sadly. "Hard as rubber."

She laughed, feeling her own tension ease. "I've had a lot of practice."

"I'd ask you to give your recipe to Kath, but she'd only mangle it."

She glanced up at him, then stared fixedly at her plate. Damn the man! she thought a bit wildly. How could he look so ridiculously wistful about an omelet? And she wasn't really surprised to hear herself speak. "I get up early every day, and it's just as easy to fix two breakfasts as one."

She was so grimly unsettled by that point that if Rafe had reminded her a second time her job wasn't cooking, she wouldn't have said another word about the subject. Rafe, however, did no such thing.

"In that case," he said solemnly, "I'll play the fiddle at your wake."

Maggie smiled. Getting up to take her plate to the sink, she said only, "Two questions."

"Which are?"

"Can you play the fiddle?"

"I'll learn. Second question?"

"What makes you think you'll be around for my wake? In the nature of things, you know, you'll predecease me."

"The chances of that are even stronger than nature allows. My mother used to say I was born to be hanged."

Maggie decided not to comment on that. Before she could say anything at all, a small flap at the base of the back door, unnoticed by her until then, swished open to admit a black cat. The cat sauntered across the kitchen with an air of belonging and leaped briefly to the counter before taking a second jump to land neatly on Rafe's shoulder.

He had gotten to his feet to carry his own plate to the sink, and now stared at his passenger. "And where have you been all night?" he demanded severely.

Green eyes returned his stare for a moment, then the cat yawned widely to show an impressive set of teeth.

"Your familiar?" Maggie asked.

"A tomcat," he answered dryly. "Like me."

Rather hastily, she opened the dishwasher and began loading it. "What's his name?" After a somewhat prolonged silence, she looked back at Rafe to find him clearly torn between reluctance and amusement. "His name's a secret?"

"No." Rafe sighed. "But after your remark, his name's a bit too apt."

"What is it?"

"Merlin."

Maggie closed the dishwasher and straightened, fighting to keep an expressionless face. "I see. Sure he isn't your familiar?"

"He's not even my cat. At least—I suppose he is, but it was his decision rather than mine. He showed up late one night about a year ago. It was storming, and I let him in. He's been here ever since."

"It's supposed to be good luck for a black cat to adopt you, especially during a storm. Why'd you name him Merlin?"

"I don't know." He looked at the cat bemusedly. "It just seemed a good name for him."

"Merlin . . ." She laughed. "If you had Warlock as well as Merlin, people would begin to wonder."

"Who—or what—is Warlock?" Rafe asked as they left the kitchen by the back door and headed for the barns. Merlin continued to ride on his shoulder with the ease of an old habit; obviously he was a companionable cat whenever not out courting.

"Warlock is a horse." Maggie breathed in the early morning air with unconscious pleasure. "He's a three-time national champion, and only four years old. He's so black, his coat has a blue sheen. His only marking is a perfect white exclamation point between his nostrils. And his owner—Ted Hawkes of Blueridge Farm in Kentucky—won't sell him for love or money. Rumor has it he's been offered plenty of the latter."

"How much is plenty?" Rafe asked, studying her profile and listening to the lilt in her voice.

"Well, I heard he's been offered a quarter of a million. That isn't so uncommon for Thoroughbred racehorses, but it's a bit steep for a Walking Horse—even a champion."

"It's possible he could earn that much in winnings and stud fees, isn't it?" Rafe asked thoughtfully.

"Yes . . . if he breeds true. But the oldest colt he's sired hasn't entered the show ring yet, so who can tell?"

"What's your guess?"

Maggie was a little surprised at the question, but answered honestly. "Well, I rode him once when he was a two-year-old, and I've seen some of his foals. My best guess is that he'll be a champion for years yet, and stand at stud well into old age. If he remains sound, that is."

"Seems like he'd be a real asset for any stud farm," Rafe commented casually.

Barn number four, Maggie's domain, showed careful planning in layout, as did the other barns. It was a T-shaped structure. The crossbar of the T was an indoor training ring—necessary in this land of intense heat and strong sun—fifty feet wide and nearly a hundred feet long, with a firm and well-kept sand floor. The barn proper was composed of a hall fifteen feet wide with roomy stables on each side, along with a large tack and equipment room and a feed room. Dutch doors gave access to each stable, and the north row of stables also had Dutch doors opening out into individual paddocks to the rear. High above along the rows of stables and adding insulation against the heat, lofts were stacked with sweet-smelling hay. At each end of both barn and training ring, also high above, were huge fans to circulate air and help to cool the buildings.

It was a trainer's dream, and Maggie couldn't believe it *was* her domain. She was speechless.

Until she met Figure.

Entering the shaded coolness of the barn hall from the equally cool training ring, Maggie stopped at Rafe's side to stare at the gray-and-white animal barring their way. Rheumy brown eyes stared at her balefully and long ears swiveled around to lie flat in unprovoked anger.

Merlin hissed, obviously annoyed, and leaped

from Rafe's shoulder to stalk back the way they'd come.

Maggie, having been around show horses all her life, knew a mascot when she saw one. Often high-strung horses became attached to stable companions and tended to remain calm in their presence. Older horses, ponies, donkeys, goats, cats, and dogs were sometimes so important to the show horses that they even accompanied them from show to show, riding companionably in the trailers with their friends.

"Mascot?" Maggie asked, gazing at the donkey.

Rafe sighed. "He thinks so. Maggie, meet Figure."

She sent Rafe a half-incredulous, half-amused look. "You named him after the famous Morgan?"

He chuckled. "No. One of the definitions of the word is 'a well-known personage.' That's what he thinks he is."

She laughed softly. "He does have a certain air about him."

"Doesn't he? And I hate to do this to you, but I'm afraid you're stuck with him—at least as long as you're training Diablo."

"They're buddies?"

Rafe nodded. "I had Tom move Diablo here early this morning, and Figure came with him. Sorry, Maggie. He's an ill-tempered old mountain burro and hates every living thing except that stallion."

Maggie was unperturbed. "Oh, we'll get along."

"He bites," Rafe warned.

"He won't bite me," she said calmly.

And that, Rafe found to his astonishment, turned out to be more than true: By the end of the day the damn burro was following her around like a puppy.

Rafe was even more astonished when he realized he was doing the same thing.

Three

Rafe had shown Maggie around the ranch,
introducing her to everyone. They wound up at her
barn, and Maggie had immediately gone to work.
Getting out her own two horses, she saddled them
while talking with apparent casualness to the people Rafe had hired to work with her. After working
both horses herself, she then asked all six of her
new apprentices to mount, two at a time, until all
of them had ridden each horse. Only one of the riders was familiar with gaited horses; the other five
particularly benefited from Maggie's patience and the
beautiful training of her horses.

By lunchtime she told Rafe that the two young
women, Lisa and Pat, as well as Tyler, one of the
young men, would be showing Shamrock horses
by the following year. The remaining three men—
Russell, Mike, and Brian—would need more time
before showing.

"But Brian has shown gaited horses before," Rafe said.

"Did he win?" Maggie asked, though it wasn't really a question.

They were walking up the lane to the house for lunch, and Rafe felt his respect for the woman growing as he looked down at her. "No, I don't think he did. How'd you know that?"

She frowned a little, gazing ahead. "He's heavy-handed and overcues, and his seat is too forward. He's also too ready to use his whip. He may not work out, Rafe."

He nodded and said, "Your decision."

She was, Rafe quickly found out, a very decisive lady. She also possessed the ability to command—and to do so without rousing even a flicker of resentment. By the end of the first day her apprentices had been briskly assigned duties, and all were clearly respectful of both her authority and her knowledge.

She also was not a woman who gave up easily or delegated the tricky or hard work to others. Watching her during the next few days, Rafe noted that she unerringly recognized both the horses—and the people—who needed the most careful handling. Rather than simply give up on Brian, she spent a great deal of time working patiently to correct his riding problems. And when a temperamental young Saddlebred showed off a few dangerous tricks, she handled him herself until some of his nasty habits were broken.

Rafe found his gaze drawn to her whenever she was within sight, and found himself searching for her when he couldn't see her. He invented questions to ask her just to hear her voice—and to get her to focus on him rather than her work. He mocked himself silently for his inability to hold her attention. Rafe, the charming rake! In a horse race—he lost out to the horses.

He asked himself honestly if the attraction could possibly be one-sided. But Maggie seemed to be too aware of him for that to be the case. She avoided any physical contact with him, he noticed, and that was not so with everyone else. With her apprentices casual contact seemed just that—casual.

The hell of it was, Rafe thought, he could make her aware of him. But the tactics he'd have to use—wanted to use—would quite effectively destroy his claim that he never got involved with women on the ranch.

He spent every spare moment he was able to find or steal watching her work in the training ring, to the point that Tom Graham—on whom the burden of Rafe's daily work fell—fiercely demanded a raise.

Both sheepish and startled by this reminder of his responsibilities, Rafe murmured only, "Sure, Tom."

The foreman pushed his hat to the back of his head and stared at his boss for a long and, to Rafe, uncomfortable moment. Then he began to laugh, crinkling the fine network of wrinkles at the corners of his faded blue eyes. "Hell. That little lady's got you corralled."

Rafe assumed a total deafness and continued to observe Maggie riding Diablo in the ring.

Tom, who had watched Rafe grow up, leaned against the gate and gazed into the ring himself. "She's a damn fine horsewoman," he said. After a sidelong glance at his boss he added, "And ambitious, I'd say. Wants her own place. Not the kind who'd marry to get it either."

Rafe sighed, abandoning his deafness. "Yeah, I know. And she's about half convinced I'm the playboy of the Western world."

"So what're you goin' to do about it?"

Frowning, Rafe considered the question. Again. He'd thought of little else for days now. What *was* he going to do about it? In spite of all his efforts Maggie was wary of him. They were rarely alone together. Breakfast was a time she clearly made a point of putting quickly behind them, and she always went to her room immediately after dinner.

Rafe knew himself to be hotheaded, but he was finding himself hot-blooded as well. These last nights had been pure hell. He had also grown increasingly nervous about Kathleen's inability to hide her matchmaking hopes for him. Sooner or later Maggie was bound to notice the housekeeper's misty-eyed looks and wistful sighs.

Kathleen was a potential problem. Rafe thought about that for a moment, then pushed it to the back of his mind, confident he'd come up with something sooner or later. He turned his attention again to the slender woman astride the gleaming devil-horse.

He knew himself to be a patient man in most regards, but too much proud blood flowed in his veins to allow him to wait patiently for the woman he wanted to rid herself of misconceptions and mistrust. Especially while most of her attention seemed fixed on her job.

"Boss?"

Rafe turned to find Tom gazing at him with an expression somewhere between uneasiness and amusement. "Boss, you aren't goin' to do somethin' crazy, are you?"

Straightening from the gate, Rafe grinned at his

foreman. "Crazy? Well, the rational approach hasn't gotten me very far, has it?"

Tom nearly groaned. "Rafe, the last time I saw you in this mood, all hell broke loose!"

"That," Rafe said cheerfully, "is a lie. I was in complete control of the situation."

"Tell that to your brothers." Tom was disgusted. "They're the ones had to bail you out of jail!"

Ignoring this, Rafe said only, "Do me a favor and get Saladin out, will you?" He looked at his watch, murmuring to himself, "Ah. . . . Just in time."

Tom seemed about to question, then shook his head and strode off, grumbling audibly.

Rafe waited until Maggie and Diablo passed near him before calling out, "Can that brute be trusted around another stallion?"

Maggie pulled up and regarded him quizzically. "I think so," she answered. "Why?"

"You've spent all your time here so far in the barns. You should see more of Shamrock." He swung open the gate without waiting for her response. "C'mon."

She rode Diablo slowly from the ring and out through the barn, following the tall, lean figure striding ahead. She glanced aside only once to watch Figure trot from his open stall and take up a "heel" position at Diablo's flank, and felt more than heard the stallion rumble a greeting to his small friend. Then she looked once more at Rafe.

Rafe Delaney, she had found, was not an easy man to ignore—even when he didn't call attention to himself. Rafe drew people as the sun drew flowers to lean toward it. She had watched him unobtrusively during every day here, noticing that nearly all of the employees at Shamrock found some reason to speak briefly to him as often as possible. Men and women alike seemed to bask in the warmth of his grin. Every last one of them, she thought, would have done anything short of murder for him—and possibly even that.

It made Maggie very nervous. He was a devastatingly charismatic man, and he was beginning to haunt her dreams. His reputation still made her uneasy, even though common sense told her a great deal of that had to be malicious gossip and wishful thinking. She kept reminding herself that he was her boss and nothing more. Nothing. And he hadn't so much as hinted that she was anything other than an employee he valued because of her ability.

Maggie was unnerved to discover that, for the first time in her career, being valued for her skill alone was not enough. She was disgusted with herself, and morbidly anxious not to betray her growing fascination with the man she still desperately wanted to pigeonhole as "boss."

And now she held Diablo to a slow walk, more concerned with controlling herself than him, bothered by her confused emotions. The carefully planned course of her life seemed to have run amok somehow. Her professional goals loomed nearer than she had dared to hope, but she was more than ever conscious of her lack of personal goals.

Maggie wrenched her thoughts to the here and now and focused her attention on the stallion Rafe was mounting several yards away. She had seen the horse at a distance, running free in the paddock attached to his stable. Saladin was Rafe's "personal" horse, raised and trained by him from long-legged coltish unsteadiness to magnificently graceful adulthood. A fiery chestnut, he was pure-blooded Arab from his delicate face to his arched tail, every inch of him a reminder of desert sands and hot winds.

She watched Rafe settle into the English saddle with a grace all his own, watched Saladin prance and snatch at the bit playfully, and felt an odd, unfamiliar weakening somewhere inside her. A headdress for Rafe and tassles for the horse, she thought dazedly, and the image would be of a powerful and arrogant sheikh riding out to survey his kingdom. . . .

"Ready?" he called cheerfully.

Maggie swallowed and needlessly rearranged Diablo's reins in her hands. "Ready."

Rafe led the way, cantering along the lane dividing barns, training rings, corrals, and paddocks for nearly half a mile. Figure, braying irritably, kept up with his friend, and heads turned to show grinning faces as they passed.

It was late afternoon, nearly evening, and reasonably cool, though the sun was still glaring. Hills rose all around them as they left the lane and the greener land near the San Pedro River behind them. Rafe stopped only once to open a security gate and close it behind them. Then they rode for nearly an hour across rolling land covered with the short, sparse grass that was so different from the lush eastern pastureland Maggie was used to.

Finally they followed a well-worn trail up to the top of a high hill, and she found herself gazing across a breathtaking expanse of the San Pedro Valley. The bulk of Shamrock Ranch lay to the east, the buildings seeming small in the distance, while all around sprawled the curiously wide and empty reaches of the valley. The sun cast slanting rays and shadows, an occasional cloud high above leaving its dark silhouette on the valley floor.

Maggie, caught up with her work, had not really looked at the land until now. She felt her senses open up in what was almost an agony of sudden awareness, conscious of the vastness, the raw beauty of this land. Mountains reared their stark, jutting peaks, shadows and colors changing moment by moment as the sun lowered. And the sun itself, sinking gracefully, was a brilliant light playing over a land not even man had dared to claim he had mastered.

She thought she could see forever.

"Beautiful, isn't it?"

Turning at Rafe's hushed voice, Maggie looked at him. He sat erect yet relaxed in the saddle, his hands folded and resting on the pommel. And he *was* a sheikh, Maggie thought . . . his headdress tossed aside. A king without his crown. A man gazing out over land for which his ancestors had shed blood, sweat, and tears to call their own. A land as untamed as a part of him still was.

"It gets in the blood, this land," he said, his tone still soft. "The sun bakes you and the wind parches you and the river's dry more often than not. Ride casually down into a dry wash, and a flash flood may sweep you away before you've time to hear it coming. And at night you can see lightning in the mountains, and clouds roll out over the sky in front of you only to disappear behind you, leaving the stars so near, you could put them in your pocket."

Maggie took a deep breath, only half aware of being enmeshed in a spell conjured by the lonely grandeur of this land and the unconscious, soul-deep pride of this man. She heard herself speaking, and the husky voice was not hers but was right for this place. "Did your family settle here?"

He shook his head. "Not originally. East of here roughly, in the Sulphur Springs Valley. That's where Killara is."

"Killara?" She was fascinated by the way he spoke the word, the soft brogue cloaking a curious blend of pride, contentment, and an ineffable sense of roots set deeply and immovably.

Rafe continued to gaze out over distance and time. "Killara. Old Shamus decided the place would be a new beginning, a new dawn for his family. Killara was the name of the ancestral home in Leinster Province, Ireland. That was the . . . piece of Ireland Shamus brought with him."

"He must have been an extraordinary man."

Abruptly Rafe turned his head to grin wickedly at her. "I'll say. He missed being hanged three times just by the skin of his teeth!"

Maggie laughed in spite of herself. "Good heavens, why?"

"Reiving mostly. You're Irish; you know what it means."

"Cattle rustling?" She laughed again. "Here?"

"No, in the Old Country. Smuggling too." When his horse moved restlessly, Rafe absently passed a strong hand gently over his stallion's neck. "I'm not sure whether he came west because he wanted to or had to."

"Did he tread the straight and narrow here?"

"I don't doubt he did a bit of reiving here as well," Rafe answered whimsically. "But it was a common thing then, with longhorns running wild and free for the taking. He was fairly well occupied with the Apaches, though."

"This is Apache country, isn't it? Raids?"

"For years." Rafe laughed softly. "They tried to drive him out. Stole his horses, set fire to his homestead. He rebuilt Lord knows how many times. When the other settlers took to their heels, Shamus stood firm and said he'd shoot anything with feathers, so friendlies had best be cautious how they approached the place."

"What finally happened?" she asked, fascinated.

With a meditative air he answered, "I believe several tribes finally got together and decided they were losing face. Since they couldn't get rid of Shamus, it seemed logical just to call him one of their own. He wasn't very amenable to becoming a blood brother, but it so happened that one of his sons—Joshua—had been prowling where he shouldn't have and had fallen in love with the daughter of a chief. After a bit of sparring and horse trading, Rising Star became a Delaney."

"No more raids?"

"None to speak of. I believe there was an occasional argument over the horses the Delaney boys took a great deal of pleasure in stealing back, but with a chief's daughter in the house things were pretty quiet."

Maggie gazed out over the land spread all around them, again conscious of a heightened awareness. "How exciting it must have been then," she murmured, half to herself.

Rafe looked at her, his hands tightening one over the other. She would not have been out of place then, he thought. For all her delicate appearance and tiny size, she was tempered steel within. She would have fought her way across a virgin land, then carved a home from wilderness with a will and the strength to endure.

She would not have asked another to bear her burdens or fight her battles or carry her gun.

And if an Apache raid had come with a red dawn,

even old Shamus would have felt stronger with her gun booming beside his.

Rafe took a deep breath and let it out slowly, still watching her. He felt Saladin shift beneath him, and had to force himself to relax the grip of his knees. The movement of the stallion drew Maggie's attention.

"He's a beautiful horse, Rafe."

Clearing his throat, Rafe murmured, "I thought so the first moment I saw him, staggering around banging his head and getting his legs all tangled. He has two half-brothers born within a day. I raised and trained them, then gave them to my brothers."

Maggie remembered hearing about that. "Sheikh and Shalimar, right?"

"Right. Sheikh's a black hellion—*very* suited to York. And Shalimar's a gray with the speed of the wind. Both are at Killara, since York spends most of his time at the mining camp."

"Who lives at Killara?" she asked curiously. "Your oldest brother?"

"Burke. Yes, he lives there when he isn't at the Tower in Tucson. He should be home now—that is, if he listened to York and me—taking some time away from the office."

Feeling suddenly uncomfortable at her own display of curiosity, Maggie turned her gaze back to the horizon. The sun had lowered while they talked, and shadows were lengthening as the red orb began to dip below the peaks of distant mountains. "We should start back," she said.

Rafe reined his stallion around to start back down the trail, and Maggie fell in behind. Figure, who had been grazing idly nearby, instantly took up his accustomed position beside Diablo. Once they reached the base of the hill, Rafe waited for Maggie to come up alongside him. They were walking the horses now, neither of them showing the natural inclination of stallions to fight one another.

Maggie glanced once at Rafe, then looked ahead, disturbed. It wasn't, she thought, anything she could pin down in his expression that was making her suddenly breathless. His black eyes seemed a bit brighter than usual, and his lazy smile quirked upward a bit higher on one side. Small distinctions in a very expressive face, Maggie thought. And when he spoke, his deep voice was the same as usual—almost.

"You should always wear red," he said. "Makes you come alive."

Instinctively she glanced down at her red knit shirt, then tossed a second glance his way. "Thanks," she muttered, resisting an impulse to demand if she didn't look alive without wearing red.

Rafe might have heard the silent question.

"You're so controlled, you know. So calm. It's startling what a change a little color—or animation—makes."

"Control is necessary when working with horses," she said as if reciting a well-learned proverb, and grimaced without surprise when he laughed.

But he said only, "I know it is. Never thought of taking it to extremes myself, but to each his own."

Maggie felt tension in her jaw and realized that her teeth were clenched. The wildness of this land was rousing an equal wildness in her, she decided. Why else would his comments grate so? "I get the job done, don't I?" she snapped, her anger show-

ing only in words and not in the hands firmly holding her horse's reins.

"That you do, Maggie," he agreed cheerfully.
"That you do."

For some reason his agreement grated even more
on Maggie's nerves. And when he followed up with
a critical comment, she found herself longing for a
riding crop.

"Still, it wouldn't hurt you to relax a bit. You'll be
old before your time if you're not careful."

"That's my business!" She felt a moment of horror after her outburst. Oh, Lord. What if he fired
her? She *loved* it here, more and more each day.
Her job and the country and the people. . . .
Sneaking a glance at Rafe's face, she saw he was
still smiling, and she sighed silently.

"Tell me something, Maggie." His voice was casual. "You obviously asked questions about Shamrock and the Delaneys before you took this job.
Right?"

"Yes." Her meek tone was a result of relief rather
than humility.

"What's the one most common thing you've
heard about my family, past and present?"

She didn't even have to consider. "That the
Delaneys take care of their own."

"Right." Somehow he managed to infuse that
single word with a great deal of meaning.

Relief faded into uneasiness. Maggie turned her
head to stare at his profile. "Just what," she asked
evenly, "is that supposed to mean?"

He turned to meet her eyes, his own dancing
with that devil-light of laughter and mischief.
"Just what you think it does," he answered amia-
bly. "We take care of our own, Maggie. So you see,

your welfare is very important to me. And I can't help feeling that you need to relax and enjoy life."

"I'm fine," she said flatly. "I've taken care of myself for ten years, and—"

"That was before it made a difference to me."

She felt her throat close up, and stared between Diablo's ears fixedly.

After a moment Rafe said admiringly, "Maggie, you're a woman in a million! Any other would have pounced on that remark instantly, reading all kinds of personal meanings into it. But not you. No, you just accept that I'm a concerned employer and that's all."

She felt her teeth gritting again, and uncharacteristically clapped her heels into the stallion's sides to urge him forward. Startled, Diablo leaped instantly into a gallop, angling away from the path they were following to cut across the open pastureland. Figure brayed loudly at being left behind.

"Maggie!" Rafe's voice was not bland, casual, or amiable. It was a hoarse roar packed with surging emotion.

She would have stopped, but couldn't, all her attention occupied in remaining in the saddle as her mount raced over land far more uneven than it had seemed. Twice Diablo literally dropped beneath her as undetectable dry washes appeared under his hooves, and he had to scramble wildly for steady footing. Perforce his reckless gallop slowed, but the third wash caught him unawares, and the loose sand robbed him of his balance. The stallion lurched sideways and nearly fell, throwing Maggie over his head and forcing him to leap awkwardly to avoid stepping on her.

Maggie came down hard, the sandy ground and

sparse tufts of grass no cushion, but she rolled instantly to disperse her weight more evenly. Sitting up, she rubbed her right shoulder with a muttered curse, her gaze following her horse as he slowed and turned back toward her. She was far more embarrassed than hurt, and silently ridiculed herself for the unthinking dash across land she was unfamiliar with.

Sand sprayed her as Saladin slid to a halt nearby, and she nerved herself to face Rafe's justifiable anger. The face she hesitantly looked up to see, however, held emotions other than anger. His skin was gray beneath the tan, the black eyes burning with a flickering wildness. His mouth was rigid, but she could have sworn the bottom lip quivered faintly for a flashing instant.

"That was stupid of me . . ." she began as he reached her side.

He dropped to one knee and hauled her against him, his arms holding her in a rib-crushing embrace. "I should have warned you," he said thickly. "Dammit, Maggie, don't ever do that to me again!"

Shaken by the toss and still conscious of her odd, heightened awareness, Maggie was further unsettled to find her body molding itself bonelessly to his hard form. She could feel his taut, work-hardened muscles, feel the raw power in his arms. His heart was pounding against her. One large hand held her head to his neck, and she was stingingly aware of the pulse throbbing beneath the flesh of his throat.

For a moment she remained limp and mindless, but then her instincts rose up within her, shrieking an alarm. Before she could make a move to push him away, however, his embrace gentled.

She was suddenly being cradled instead of crushed. His entire body seemed to soften and draw her within a warm hollow.

"I should have warned you," he repeated, his voice quieter but still husky. "This is an unforgiving land, Maggie, a land that gives no quarter." His cheek was pressed to her hair, and his hand slid down to rest gently at the nape of her neck. "Promise me you won't take chances again, or ride out alone until you know the land."

"I promise," she whispered, her hands lifting of their own volition to rest on his chest. She couldn't remember ever being held like this in a caring embrace. Her father had been a taciturn man, more interested in horses than in the emotional needs of his daughter, and her own driven ambition had held all others strictly at arm's length. She felt strangely cherished, and a dimly recognized part of her gloried in that unfamiliar sensation.

She forgot that he was her boss and, moreover, a man to be wary of. She forgot ambition and safety and the certainty of herself. Her consciousness tunneled, focusing only on this moment. The sandy ground beneath her knees was hard but distant, and a soft, warm breeze played over her newly aching body. Even the animals—including Figure, who had caught up with them—were still, not intruding, and the setting sun bathed them all in a reddish glow.

Rafe held her in silence, stroking her back with the same gentling touch with which he had so recently soothed his horse. And it soothed Maggie, but it also sapped her willpower and strength. Without thought she watched her hand slide from just beneath the hollow of his shoulder to where dark hair curled at the opening of his white shirt.

She saw her fingers touch that silky hair, and felt a tingle in her fingertips and an instant liquid heat being released somewhere within her.

Alarmed, she raised her head and then stilled, gazing into black eyes with lambent flames in their bottomless depths. She wanted to speak, to say something that would instantly allot them their clearly defined positions as employer and employee, but she could force no sound past her suddenly tight throat.

The hand at her nape shifted to warmly cup the side of her neck, tilting her face up, and those black eyes came nearer until they filled her vision, her thoughts.

"Maggie . . ." he breathed softly, all but inaudibly, just before his lips touched hers.

For an instant, an eternity, Maggie gave in to the giddy sensations rushing through her body. His lips hardened in desire, slanting across hers with a sudden fierce hunger, setting wildfire alight deep inside of her. She felt her body, her emotions, everything she was, swaying toward him, pulled irresistibly by a strong sense of affinity. A part of her had been waiting for this, yearning for it. It was more than desire, more than anything she'd ever known before, and fear washed cold sanity through her mind.

Violently she tore her mouth from his, and would have broken completely away from him but for the iron strength of his arms. The hold trapped without hurting, and she was powerless to escape. She met his gaze, her own fierce and wary, and for a moment felt the breath catch in her throat. There was, she saw, something not quite tame in his eyes, something hot and primitive. Then the fleeting wildness was gone, and his crooked smile dawned.

"I won't apologize," he murmured.

"I didn't expect an apology!" she snapped breathlessly, clinging to anger and telling herself that the gossips had been right after all. Rafe was scalp-hunting and nothing more, and she was no trophy.

"No," he said, "you expected a playboy. Well, Maggie love, I've decided I might as well be hanged for a sheep as a lamb."

"What?" she asked, bewildered.

Mournfully he quoted, " 'My reputation, Iago, my reputation!' "

She stared at him.

Grinning now, he said, "I've lost my reputation where you're concerned, and without even a trial either." He rose to his feet, pulling her gently up and holding both her hands in his. "I might as well take advantage of it. I don't know if I can live up to your image of a rapacious rogue, but I'm willing to try, Maggie love. Try very hard."

She had the peculiar feeling that she was being manipulated, and stared at his wide grin and the dimple that was incongruous with his otherwise rugged face. For the life of her she didn't know whether to hit him with something or to laugh.

"You're not— That is, you—you wouldn't . . ." She wasn't a stammering sort of woman, but she couldn't seem to formulate either her thoughts or her words.

"Wouldn't I? Darlin', I'm a rogue, a rake, a scoundrel. Women litter the road behind me like so much confetti. My bedroom has a revolving door. I'm trying desperately to break Don Juan's record, and—"

"I get the point!" she said crossly, still not

entirely sure how she was supposed to react to the combination of his unnerving words and bland tone of voice. "Rafe, you can't be serious!"

His eyes widened innocently. "But, love, you cringe whenever I come near—filled with visions of ravishment, I'm sure—so I just thought I'd earn the reaction."

"I do not cringe!" Maggie wanted to command him to stop using the endearments, except that she didn't want him to know she'd noticed. She'd never felt so confused or off-balance in her life. "You *said* your reputation was all a lot of hot air— vicious gossip!"

"But you believe it," he reminded her smoothly.

Baffled, she stared at him. "You said you never got involved with the women here on the ranch."

"Blarney. I decided to make an exception in your case. I changed my mind. . . . I lied." He lifted one flying brow mockingly. "Take your pick."

For a moment Maggie wondered a bit wildly just how many men boasted the name of Rafe Delaney. She seemed to have encountered at least four just during today's ride: a thoughtful man proudly aware of his land and his blood, a gentle man who had held her like a cherished thing, a fiercely passionate man, and now this devil.

It was like gazing into myriad mirrors, each reflecting a Rafe. One was the real man—but which?

"That's—that's harassment," she managed.

Clearly wounded, he explained patiently, "No, darlin', not harassment. Your job's secure no matter what happens between us. A rake I may be, but I'm not an idiot. You're too damn good a trainer to lose."

Suddenly conscious of his hands holding hers,

Maggie jerked away from his grasp. "I'll quit!" she threatened.

"No, you won't. You're no coward."

She glared at him for a full minute, then turned on her heel and stalked over to where Diablo was waiting patiently. Angry as she was, she nonetheless automatically accepted a leg up into the saddle from Rafe, and muttered almost inaudible curses as she watched him mount his own horse. Damn the man! she thought. What did he want from her? A playmate? Another scalp to dangle arrogantly from his Delaney belt?

Was her position at Shamrock worth the battle she could envision building up between her and Rafe?

Rafe observed Maggie's confusion much more closely than he allowed her to see. He was gambling, gambling on her response to him, and on her own ambition. She wouldn't leave, he thought. At least not while he could keep her off-balance and uncertain. And in the meantime he meant to take full advantage of her confusion.

Four

Riding beside Rafe as they started back to the ranch, Maggie carefully kept her gaze fixed straight ahead. She was worried and uneasy and wanted, oddly, either to laugh or to cry or to knock Rafe from his horse with a well-aimed blow . . . or *something.*

She didn't want to leave Shamrock, both because of her professional plans and because she was growing to love the place, yet her every instinct urged her to fold her tent and steal away—now, before it was too late. Rafe possessed the uncanny knack of drawing all her emotions closer to the surface, leaving her feeling unsettled and vulnerable, and that was a feeling she'd never known before. It was dangerous, she knew.

Obviously Rafe wanted nothing more than another conquest. And she wanted . . . What did she want? A secure future, her own ranch. Success. Control. She'd worked for ten years, and more years of hard work stretched ahead of her before that driving wish could come true.

It would take even longer if she left Shamrock and was forced to accept a position at a less prestigious ranch. . . .

She couldn't leave. Not just because her boss's fickle fancy had settled on her. He was a chameleon, and chameleons were creatures of change. He'd lose interest in her soon enough. Surely he'd lose interest. He could have any woman he wanted, and she was nothing special. She could keep him at arm's length until he lost interest.

Unwillingly Maggie remembered an embrace that had sapped her willpower and a kiss that had left her weak and defenseless. She swallowed hard and clenched her teeth. That, she decided, wouldn't happen again.

"You won't leave," Rafe said calmly.

The assurance in his voice very nearly provoked her, but Maggie checked her temper. "I like my job," she said as evenly as she could.

"Good. I hope you like your boss as well."

"Don't fish with me," she warned. "You wouldn't like the catch!"

He burst out laughing, a deep, lilting sound.

They had reached the pasture gate, and as soon as he opened it Maggie urged Diablo to canter down the lane to the barns. She didn't look back to see if Rafe was following, but heard his good-humored shouts to various stablehands as he passed them. She also heard him halt Saladin near barn number two, where the horse's stable was, while she rode on to number four.

Reaching her barn, Maggie swung off Diablo and removed his tack. The stallion had proved fairly tractable where women other than Maggie were concerned, even to the point of allowing the apprentice Lisa to ride him, but six years of men trying to break him had left scars. Diablo despised men and allowed none to touch him.

After carrying the saddle and bridle into the tackroom, Maggie returned to groom the stallion thoroughly. The long walk back had cooled him, so that there was no need to walk him further, but she carefully made certain he had not injured himself during that mad race across the pasture. She had just turned Diablo into his stall when Rafe strolled into the barn.

"Tomorrow," he said, "I'll take you out to see the brood mares and foals. They're pastured farther up the valley."

"I have to work," she said. Without waiting for his response, she went back into the tackroom to get her bridle and the saddle soap, then sat in the doorway to clean the gear.

Rafe leaned against the wall and watched her, still wearing that crooked, oddly dangerous smile. "I'm not about to let you work seven days a week, Maggie, and tomorrow's Saturday. You can take a few hours off. Besides, I noticed you've scheduled your people so that at least two of them are here every day."

She wanted to snap at him, but he *was* her boss. She tried to tune out his presence, listening to the sounds of Lisa and Mike working two of the Saddlebreds in the training ring and staring down at the bridle in her lap as she automatically cleaned it.

"Nearly dinnertime," Rafe said, just as the interior barn lights came on automatically with the dusk.

"Tell Kathleen not to bother with my dinner, would you, please? I have some work to finish up, so I'll fix a snack or something later." She still refused to look up at him.

After a moment he said quietly, "You don't have to keep working your two horses on your own time, Maggie."

She was surprised that he'd noticed that; she tended to ride her own horses just after breakfast or around lunchtime. "I'd rather, if you don't mind," she said evenly. "When I work for you, I'll work for you. I work for myself on my own time."

"You're a lot like this land, Maggie," he said softly. "You give no quarter."

She looked up slowly, but he was gone. She sat there for a long time, thinking. No quarter? No mercy. Was she that unyielding? So rigid there was no way for her to bend? Had the long, lonely years of hard work made her so inflexible that her every movement, every thought or action, *had* to bring her a step nearer her distant goals?

Automatically she finished cleaning the tack. Lisa and Mike brought their mounts into the hall to be unsaddled and groomed, and she spoke to them casually. She saddled and worked her two horses, calling out a cheerful good night to her two apprentices as they left the barn, but not halting her own work.

It was late when she finally left the barn after giving all the horses a final check and turning out all but the dim night-lights. She locked up the barn by closing the huge, electrically powered doors that closed off the hall and training ring, then activated the security system for the building. As she walked up the lane between the barns toward the house, all was dark and quiet, only the occasional stamp of hooves or soft nicker disturbing the silence. She turned between barns seven and eight, following the lane where it curved toward the house, familiar enough with the way by now to be unperturbed by the pitch darkness between and beyond the buildings.

She was so lost in thought that she heard nothing, and was so completely taken by surprise that only a squeak escaped her when hard arms caught her in a crushing embrace. Lips ruthlessly captured her own, kissing her with a driving passion that stole her breath. For an instant shock held her still, then she fought fiercely. But before she could do more than begin to struggle, she was free—and alone.

Breathless, Maggie peered through the darkness all around her, ears straining for the slightest sound. Nothing. Confused, she remembered the sensation of some kind of buckskinlike fringe beneath her fingers, and remembered a fleeting glimpse of what must have been a very tall man. No, she thought, bewildered, not just tall. There had been something on his head.

She straightened, then grabbed quickly at her neck. Something was tickling her, something protruding from the V neckline of her knit shirt. Visions of spiders and other unpleasant things faded as her fingers grasped the object and pulled it from her shirt. She stepped out of the inky blackness of shadows, she heard her own voice say incredulously, "A *feather*?"

Glancing warily around as she continued toward the house, Maggie toyed with the feather bemusedly and attempted to collect her thoughts. She tried to decide if there had been anything familiar about her attacker, her suspicions instantly focused on Rafe. She didn't know *why* he would do such a ridiculous thing, but the devil-light in his eyes made it at least plausible.

But something was nagging at her, something she had sensed more than seen. She was somehow convinced it hadn't been Rafe. Who then? And why?

Her stride quickened as she neared the house. If it *had* been Rafe, he couldn't possibly have returned to the house and changed from that buckskin outfit—or whatever it had been—so quickly. She entered the house through the kitchen, relieved to find it empty, and hurried on toward the den.

Rafe was there, hanging up the phone as she paused in the doorway. He was dressed casually in jeans and a black shirt unbuttoned halfway down his chest, and showed absolutely no signs of having just run several hundred yards or changed in a hurry.

Black suited him, she thought fleetingly. He looked more devillike than usual tonight, even without the dancing light of mockery in his eyes.

He rose to his feet as he looked up and saw her. "You worked late tonight. Maggie, you really shouldn't—"

"How long have you been here?" she interrupted, not caring whether he'd consider the question impertinent.

His brows rose quizzically. "If you mean here in the den—a couple of hours. If you mean here in the house—since I left the barns. Why do you ask?"

She frowned at him, playing absently with the feather. "Oh . . . no reason. I just wondered."

He nodded toward her hands. "Where'd you get the feather?"

She took a deep breath and let it out slowly. "I found it."

He continued to look quizzical, but shrugged and allowed the subject to drop. "Are you hungry, or would you rather unwind a bit first?"

"I was going to my room—"

"Why don't you sit down and relax for a while? I promise not to pounce," he added dryly. "Tonight anyway."

Flushing, she moved past him to the couch. She sat down with a bit less grace than usual, suddenly rattled—and not because he'd asked her to remain in the room. Passing by him, she had caught the scent of his after-shave, and she realized then why she had felt so certain that rough kiss had not come from him. Rafe's after-shave—more familiar to her than she'd realized—was a very pleasant musky scent. What she had sensed fleetingly during the dark embrace had been the sharp scent of cinnamon.

Not Rafe. *Who?*

They talked casually for a while, Maggie responding absently. Then she pleaded weariness and escaped to her room. She wasn't hungry, only bewildered, and her dreams were filled with faceless Indians.

Rafe sat in the den for a long time after Maggie left, thinking. The frustration over having made no headway in persuading her to trust him had translated itself into recklessness, and Rafe knew from long experience that while that daring mood held him, he was very apt to act without thinking.

It had not been a conscious decision to play the part Maggie expected of him. He had intended only to tease, cajole, or trick her into relaxing a bit and thinking of something other than her work. But her heedless dash across terrain dangerous to anyone who didn't know it had scared the hell out of him, and his embrace had gotten out of hand.

After that his own particular devil had prodded him to play the part of a rake. He didn't know if it would work. Her reaction to his sudden turnabout had delighted him. She'd been rattled and off-balance, uncertain. And her threat to leave had been more automatic, he thought, than decisive.

But what heartened him more than anything else had been her response to his kiss. The fire he'd suspected Maggie possessed was there, lurking just beneath her cool exterior, and he now knew that passion as well as temper could set it alight.

It was more than a beginning.

Rafe was groping in the dark, but he had a strong feeling that a declaration of love from him would frighten her just as much as the rakish attentions of a so-called heartbreaker. Maggie had stood alone too long to be at ease with the thought of allowing someone else into her life.

So what he had to do, in essence, was to slide into her life without appearing to be a serious threat.

He could act with the best of them. And no one could pull out the stops or chew the scenery like a Delaney.

Maggie didn't have a chance.

He leaned forward to pick up the feather she'd left on the coffee table. As he passed it through his fingers he began to chuckle.

Throughout the following morning Maggie

brooded over her mysterious assailant, saying nothing to anyone about the episode until lunchtime. Most of the workers on Shamrock tended to pack their lunches and eat within the coolness of the barn halls, and Maggie and her staff were no exception. Rafe had been kept busy all morning at the far end of the compound over-seeing the shipment of several groups of horses going out to new owners.

Only Russell and the two girls, Pat and Lisa, were here today, and Russell had wolfed down his lunch and gone to help load some Arabians into the vans. Maggie was alone with the young women as they ate. She was trying to think of some casual way to broach the subject of strangely dressed men with strange habits when a giggling comment from Lisa made it unnecessary.

"Marion said the bandit came back last night."

Maggie looked up from her sandwich, thinking of Marion, the brisk, cheerful Arabian trainer she had met. "Bandit? What bandit?"

Lisa's green eyes widened with amusement. "The Shamrock kissing bandit. Isn't that great?"

"*What?*"

Both Lisa and Pat laughed at Maggie's incredu-lous wail, and Lisa explained.

"Yeah, that's what she told me. Nobody's ever gotten a good look, but it seems he's an Apache—or wants to be one—and he shows up here every spring. He steals kisses. I love it!" Lisa was from Chicago, and was still newly delighted at being in the Southwest. The history of the area fascinated her.

"Are you trying to tell me," Maggie said slowly, "that there's some madman running around at night dressed up like an Indian and kissing women?"

Lisa giggled again. "According to Marion—and she's been here for years."

Maggie tuned out the remainder of the conversation as her apprentices argued over possible identities, but she noticed that Rafe's name had not even been mentioned. She finished her lunch and left barn four to wander along the lane. She was thinking about the Shamrock "kissing bandit" and felt torn between incredulity and amusement. Of all the ridiculous—

Rafe approached her just then, riding a big, muscled Quarter horse and leading another one. "Come on, Maggie love. We're going to see the mares and foals!"

She looked around hastily, flushing at his somewhat loud and cheerful hail and worried at what others might think. There were plenty of people within earshot, but all seemed to have gone suddenly deaf, and Maggie's anxious gaze revealed only stony faces holding vast indifference.

It didn't reassure her.

"Stop calling me that!" she hissed, swinging aboard the horse he'd brought for her.

Rafe only grinned and tossed her a Western hat that was a smaller version of the one he wore. "Wear this, darlin'," he ordered, ignoring her command. "It's the middle of the day and you aren't used to this dry heat yet."

She clapped the hat on her head and glared at him, but had to grit her teeth to hold back a begrudging laugh. Damn the man, she thought. He was incorrigible!

He was, she rapidly found, worse than incorrigible. He kept them at a steady walk down the lane and talked to her blithely, sprinkling endearments throughout the conversation and occasionally tossing a laughing comment to people they passed. He made it quite clear he didn't give a damn who heard him addressing his new trainer as if she were his lover. In fact, he seemed to be taking pains to instill that belief in everyone within earshot.

When they left the barns far behind and reached an enormous pasture where the mares and foals were kept, Rafe dismounted and ground-tied his horse before coming to her side.

"We can walk from here," he said.

Gazing down at him, Maggie strongly mistrusted the gleam in his black eyes. "We can ride," she said firmly, abruptly conscious that they were virtually in the middle of nowhere with only horses for company.

Smiling crookedly, he reached up to grip her waist and pull her effortlessly from the horse. She gasped as she felt the length of his hard body, knowing he'd deliberately let her slide against him. She found her hands gripping his shoulders, and wondered wildly why the barriers of their clothing felt like nothing. Nothing at all.

"Rafe . . ."

"Do you know," he said huskily, "just how lovely you are?" He pulled the hat from her head and hung it on her saddle's horn, then toyed with one of her ponytails. "The sun turns your hair to golden honey, and makes your eyes sparkle. And you have such a beautiful smile. You rarely smile at me, lass. Do you know that?"

She wanted to escape his hold. At least she thought she did. But her legs refused to obey her and her hands clung to his shoulders with no will of her own. "I—I thought we were going to look at the horses," she said, aware of the unevenness of her voice.

"Horses." His smile grew even more crooked, and something like regret stirred in his eyes. "Sometimes I've wished I were a horse, Maggie. Then I'd have all your attention. I'd feel your hands stroking me, and hear your soft voice praising me. And you'd look at me with a smile in your eyes." His laugh was quiet and faintly self-mocking. "Does that sound self-centered? It is, I know. But I feel that way about you. I want all your time, and all your attention."

"Rafe, you—"

"I want to hold you." His arms tightened. "And kiss you." Warm lips feathered across her jaw. "I want to see your eyes look at me with desire, and feel your hands touching me. Is it so wrong of me, Maggie, to want that?"

She couldn't answer, couldn't find the words or the breath for them. And when his head lowered and blotted out the sun, she couldn't find the strength even to turn her face aside.

His kiss was tentative at first, warm and seeking, undemanding. Her knees became weak, and her lips parted with a need beyond any stopping, beyond all reason. She could feel the power of his shoulders beneath her fingers as he pulled her even closer until his body branded its contours on her own.

A shudder passed through Rafe and his mouth hardened, becoming hungry and demanding as she responded. He felt her hands slide up around his neck, knocking his hat away when her fingers twined in his hair. The desire that had tormented his days and nights burst suddenly into flame, rushing through his body like wildfire. Caution went spinning away, and there was only this relentless, torturing need of her.

"Maggie . . ." His voice was a hoarse gasp as his lips left hers to plunder the satiny flesh of her neck. When her head fell back to allow his exploration, his heart smothered him with its pounding.

Maggie's horse, impatient, nudged them violently just then, causing them both to stagger. Her wits recalled, Maggie pushed away from Rafe, bemused to realize her hands had been locked in his hair. Nothing in her experience had taught her how to handle this situation, and she could only stare at him as she tried to control her ragged breathing.

For the first time in his life Rafe could have struck a horse in anger. But when he looked at Maggie's strained expression, he realized that the interruption had not been as untimely as his tormented body felt it to be. He drew a deep breath and brushed his knuckles lightly down her flushed cheek, striving for humor to leash his own desire.

"What you do to me," he said roughly, "ought to be illegal." Then, without giving her time to respond, he took her hand and led her toward the horses they'd come to see.

It was difficult to recapture the earlier light mood, but surrounded by curious, friendly mares and foals, Maggie felt her tension gradually fall away. And Rafe waited for that before he suggested they return to the barns.

He had no intention of pushing Maggie into a corner from which the only escape was flight—or a confrontation neither of them was ready for.

*　　*　　*

During the following days Maggie was almost continually torn between wary anger and inner laughter. That was when Rafe was being a verbal rogue. When the cheerful, caressing words became equally cheerful, caressing actions, she didn't know what she felt.

Whether by accident, design, or plain experience, he was always careful to stop just short of the mark. She was never able to get angry enough to hit him or to leave, just angry enough to indulge in some pretty colorful swearing.

Bewildered and unsettled, she had to cope with sudden kisses on the back of her neck, with abrupt hugs, when she thought she was alone. There were playful tugs on her ponytails or braids, and he began swinging her up into his arms in order to put her on a horse instead of offering the traditional leg up. When he was around, that is—and he was almost always around.

And, she realized, those devil-black eyes were watching her with an intensity never hidden by light words or easy smiles. His behavior might be carelessly flirtatious, but his eyes told her it was no game.

He didn't interfere actively with her work, but when she wasn't on a horse she was in danger of being forced to cope with his devilish attentions. At first Maggie worried about what everyone on the ranch was thinking, but after observing bystanders of the little scenes, she began to smell a conspiracy.

Never, she decided mutinously, had there been so obvious an outbreak of mass blindness and deafness. There was never so much as a giggle at any of Rafe's outrageous flirting, and any observing eyes went opaque and distant whenever he picked her up or hugged her.

And it didn't help that the infamous kissing bandit had grabbed her twice after late working sessions, catching her offguard in spite of herself with kisses that left her shaking and bewildered.

Two men who affected her like that?

Both times she had found Rafe innocently at the house.

Curiously he made no attempt to take advantage of their time alone together in the house. He was friendly and companionable, but no more, and *that* unsettled her too.

And she again encountered the mirror-Rafe that she had first met on a hilltop overlooking the valley.

She was leaning against a fence, watching a more than usually spectacular sunset.

Although Rafe moved like a cat or a hunting brave, she had developed a built-in radar where he was concerned and felt him approach. She tensed, expecting one of his sudden hugs or kisses. But he only leaned against the fence beside her, his gaze fixed on the brilliant horizon.

"I never tire of looking at it," he murmured.

She tore her gaze from his profile and stared blindly forward. "I . . . can see how you wouldn't. It's always different."

"Ever-changing," he agreed quietly. "Has this land gotten into your blood, Maggie?"

She wanted to say no, wanted to boast that she could pull up stakes and move at any moment. She wanted to consider this place only a setting for her work and so, temporary. She wanted to believe that she could turn her back and walk away with no tugs at her heart or mind. But the truth

overbore her wishes, and the feeling was so powerful, it nearly hurt. Did hurt. She ached inside with
the knowledge that this land, this place, would
always be with her—wherever she went.

And a fleeting realization told her this man
would also go with her.

Maggie felt his gaze on her, and nodded. *The
land . . . think only of the land!* her mind
shrieked. "I've never . . . been anywhere like this
before," she managed to say.

"Or never looked?" His tone was gentle.

She nodded again, feeling the web of his spell
enmesh her as they had on the hilltop. "Never
looked, I guess. I was always too busy. You know—"
Her laugh was without humor. "I've been to
Madison Square Garden several times, and I've
never really looked at New York. I've flown over the
Grand Canyon—and never looked." She turned
blind eyes to him, suddenly aware of a strange
grief. "I never looked. How did I let that happen?"

It was the bewildered dejection of a child,
unthinking emotion, and Rafe responded
instantly. He drew her into his arms, holding her
quietly, not questioning. He held her while she
silently absorbed the bereavement of having been
so single-minded she had not even cared to gaze at
one of nature's masterpieces.

That realization haunted her for days, even
though Rafe never alluded to it. Instead, he
reverted to his rakish behavior the following day,
making her laugh and swear in spite of herself.

A few days later Maggie recaptured her earlier
image of being in a funhouse and standing in the
hall of mirrors. Each mirror reflected a Rafe, each
face subtly—or not so subtly—different from the
rest. She thought of that image because she found

herself staring at the roguish, devilish Rafe in the flesh. He had her cornered—literally—in the tackroom.

"Rafe, stop it!" She had gotten over her fear of losing her temper with the boss. He might fire her if she stole all his horses, she'd decided, but otherwise she was safe.

"Now, Maggie love, you shouldn't run from me." His black eyes were gleaming brightly.

"I've been meaning to ask," she said hastily, "why is the shamrock your family's symbol? That's the logo of all the Delaney concerns, isn't it?" She was trying to edge carefully out of his reach while keeping his mind occupied. Humor the madman, Maggie told herself.

"That was old Shamus's idea," Rafe said, stepping sideways neatly and cutting off her escape. "Because his luck came in threes or multiples of three. I've already told you he missed being hanged three times. And he had nine sons. And his first name had six letters."

Maggie unobtrusively eyed the space to Rafe's left. Big enough to escape through? "Ironic," she said chattily, "that the present generation is three."

"Isn't it?" he murmured cordially. "Old Shamus might have planned it."

She gathered herself for the attempt. "And is it true that all the Delaneys came home, so to speak? Someone said there was a graveyard at Killara—" She made a break for it.

Uncannily anticipating her, Rafe moved smoothly to intercept. Holding her quite securely in his arms, he said in a calm voice, "Yes, there's a graveyard. And all the Delaneys have come home. Except one."

"Uh . . . who was that?" she asked, staring fixedly at the unfastened third button of his blue shirt and the curling black hair just beside the button. She was trying very hard not to giggle. Or punch him in the chest. She wasn't sure which.

"William Delaney," he told her affably. "He's one of the verifiable black sheep in our history. Instead of treading the straight and narrow, he decided on a life of crime. Sadly he wasn't very successful. He's buried in Tombstone, on Boot Hill."

"Fancy that." She cleared her throat. "And no one offered to . . . uh, bring him home?"

"Burke thinks he should be buried at Killara. York thinks the choice was old Bill's, and he obviously made it."

"And what do you think?" Maggie had the odd feeling she was becoming hypnotized by that button. She felt light-headed. Of course, it couldn't be because the length of his body was pressed against hers. That was ridiculous.

"Me?" Rafe reflected at some length, as if he had all the time in the world. "Well, I think it's a dandy thing to have a relative buried at Boot Hill. Makes for interesting dinner-table conversation."

Maggie bit her bottom lip. "Oh," she acknowledged unsteadily.

"Indeed. Now, Maggie love, have we finished talking? Or are there any other little historical tidbits you'd like to know about?"

"Hey, Rafe, are you— Oh. Uh, 'scuse me." Russell backed hastily out of the tackroom, his face already beginning to assume the consistency of stone.

Maggie let her forehead fall briefly against Rafe's chest. "My reputation," she nearly wailed. "You've shot it all to hell!"

"He didn't see a thing," Rafe said soothingly, maddeningly.

She lifted her head as her teeth came together with an audible snap. "How much are you paying them not to see anything?" she demanded irately.

Rafe looked wounded. "They're blind for the love of me, Maggie lass," he drawled. "Deaf for the love of me. They'd do *anything* for the love of me. Now *you*, on the other hand—"

With great deliberation and malice aforethought Maggie brought her booted heel down on Rafe's booted toe. Freed, she backed away a couple of steps and gazed impersonally at Rafe, sitting on a low chest of drawers and nursing his foot while his curses tinted the air.

"That," he finally said coherently, "was unfair, love."

"You have the superior strength," she said sweetly. "I'll lay claim to the superior cunning."

Rafe lowered his foot to the floor and leaned forward slightly. His black eyes began to gleam brighter than ever. "I should have warned you, lass," he said softly. "Never challenge a Delaney. We don't give up."

She glared at him. "Even a Delaney," she said witheringly, "should know when to give up on a lost cause!"

"We never give up. Remember the Alamo!"

"That was Texas!"

"It's the meaning that counts."

She wanted to snatch a handful of bridles off their pegs and throw them at him. "You," she told him, "should be locked up. You're dangerous!"

"That's the nicest thing you've ever told me," he said, deeply moved.

Maggie let out a sound somewhere between a

snarl and a laugh, turned on her heel, and stalked from the tackroom, muttering to herself. She was still muttering when she realized she'd walked the length of the compound and was leaning against a fence beside Tom Graham, watching a Thoroughbred hunter being worked over jumps.

". . . elevator doesn't go to the top floor. Crazy. Loco. All the sand's sifted from his bucket. He's a few bricks short of a full load. He's got so much blarney in him, it's spilling over the edges. . . ."

Tom chuckled. "The boss?"

She gave him a look of mock astonishment. "You mean, you aren't blind and deaf like the rest of the peons?"

His faded blue eyes twinkled at her. "Not me. It's too much fun to watch and listen."

"It isn't funny, Tom!" She'd felt comfortable with the foreman from their first introduction, and found it easy to talk to him.

"Isn't it?" He sent her an oblique look. "Heard you laughing more often these days."

That stopped Maggie, but only for a moment. "The point is," she elaborated, "the man's making a fool out of me! And I have to take it because he's my employer."

Tom turned to her, abruptly grave. "Rafe wouldn't like to hear you say that. And you don't really believe it yourself."

Her eyes fell before his steady gaze. "No. No, I suppose not. But I want to stay here."

"You could stop Rafe with a word." Tom was staring straight ahead again, his face expressionless.

Maggie, too, was staring into the ring. She felt abruptly, strangely, shaken. Because she knew he was right. She could stop Rafe with a word. All she had to do was tell him no.

No, I won't be your latest playmate. No, I won't be your mistress. No, I won't wake up one morning in your bed. No. Just no. Don't bother me anymore. You're my boss and nothing more. No.

It had never been put into words between them. He had never said, quite simply, "I want you." And she had never said no.

She felt her throat close up. Why hadn't she said no? She would rage at him, evade him, even avoid him. But she had never turned to him and said simply, "I don't want that." Why?

Because it would have been a lie.

Maggie forcefully held herself still and silent, hardly conscious of the man beside her. It would have been a lie. There was a secret part of her that would carry Rafe with her all the days of her life. His would be the face she would always see in her dreams, and his kisses would make every other man's pale by comparison.

Rafe's pursuit had been, for the most part, a teasing thing. Playful, but not quite a game. But Maggie knew with an awful sense of finality that if he carried her off to his bed, she would not put up even a token resistance. She could withstand his teasing flirtation, but when those devil-black eyes gazed at her with passion, she would be lost.

She took a deep breath and silently left Tom's side. Away from the ring, she stood for a moment alone in the bright sunlight. Completely alone. A distant buzz caught her vague attention, and she lifted her head to watch a helicopter approach the ranch. It landed at some distance from the training rings and barns on the concrete pad she'd noticed days before, the shamrock logo visible even far away.

She felt more than heard Rafe, and half turned to

see him striding up the lane toward the helicopter. He flashed a grin at her and waved as he passed, calling out something she wasn't at all sure she heard correctly.

"Going to hell. See you later!"

Bemused, she watched him pause a moment beside the man in coveralls who had climbed out of the helicopter, then the other man walked away and Rafe got into the aircraft alone. She saw the helicopter lift and fly off toward the north. Hell, she mused. He was going to hell? And he'd be back later. Only a Delaney, she thought, could sound so sure of that.

And she had an almost uncontrollable urge to sink down in the sandy dirt and laugh herself silly.

Five

The house seemed lonely that night. It was lonely.
And the emptiness of the place gave Maggie too
much time to think. She occupied herself in
teaching—or trying to teach—Kathleen how to
make a baked chicken dish Maggie had often made
for her father. The housekeeper was willing, but
amazingly inept, and since she kept saying things
like "Mr. Rafe will soon be home again," it was just
too much.

It was also too much sometime later that evening
when Maggie found herself curled up in Rafe's
favorite chair, and realized she had snuggled up to
the cushion because it bore his scent.

Swearing, she went to bed.

Being no more curious than average, she
assured herself, Maggie cornered Tom at the crack
of dawn the next morning and threatened death by
inches unless he told her what "hell" Rafe had

flown off to the day before. Thoroughly cowed, he told her: Hell's Bluff, the Delaney mining town where York lived.

Hell's Bluff. It figured, she thought.

She tried very hard all morning to convince herself to leave. She really tried. She kept her people and her horses busy, cleaned tack that didn't need cleaning, and rode two Arabians as a favor to Marion. She drove her Jeep out to the cottage being readied for her, faintly surprised to find the work still in the early stages but instantly in love with the little house. She worked both of her personal horses and gave half a dozen of the surprised ranch horses baths. Then she seized a pitchfork and began mucking out a stable until one of the maintenance men took it away from her with a laughing comment about union rules.

By the end of the day Maggie was still at the ranch. Exhausted and inclined to talk to herself, but still there. She'd been conscious of the sound of a helicopter very early in the day, but had stubbornly refused to go have a look . . . or greet Rafe . . . if it was Rafe. But she discovered she was walking more quickly than usual as she neared the house.

She didn't see Rafe, and slipped quietly into the house, heading for her rooms and a shower. After dressing, she glanced out the sliding glass doors leading to the veranda, and saw a figure beyond the pool. After gazing for a moment, undecided, she finally slid the door open and made her way out there.

He was leaning against the fence watching the sunset. He must have had pretty good radar, too, she thought, because he turned before she made a sound.

Rafe had deliberately not gone in search of Maggie when he'd returned from Hell's Bluff. He had wanted her to seek him out, something in him needing that evidence that she'd missed him—at least a little. He felt his heart leap when he turned and saw her, and he forgot, for the moment, what he looked like.

Maggie stopped and stared at him. Her gaze meandered from his head to his boots. Along the way, she found a truly glorious black eye, a wide Band-Aid over his nose, and knuckles that were considerably scraped and bruised. He also looked as if he'd had little or no sleep. When her eyes lifted again to meet his, she saw that there was a sheepish expression showing on the part of his face that wasn't multicolored or bandaged.

And she just couldn't resist.

"Had a fight with the devil and lost?"

Rafe narrowed his good eye at her. "I came back, didn't I? A Delaney never loses!"

"What does the devil look like?" she asked.

"Worse. A lot worse." He lifted a hand to tenderly finger his nose. "But I broke my nose again, dammit."

Maggie bit the inside of her cheek. "Did you go to hell just to get into a fight?"

"No," he answered patiently. "I went because York called. The fight came later."

"Ah." Maggie nodded wisely. "Well, I'd say you got your just deserts."

"You don't even know what it was about."

"I don't have to. If ever a man deserved thrashing . . ."

He winced. "Don't yell at me, please, lass."

"Devil get you drunk too?" she asked, unfeeling.

"No, that came later." Rather hastily, he added, "I'm feeling bruised and battered and vulnerable."

Maggie reminded herself that Rafe was a born actor. She had told herself that repeatedly over the last week. But he *did* look vulnerable, rather wistful and pathetic and—damn the man!—it *got* to her.

"You should put a steak on that eye," she said, her voice as brisk as she could make it.

"I was going to," he said vaguely.

She took his arm and turned him toward the house. "Well, come on then."

Very meek, Rafe allowed himself to be led into the house and shooed into his den. A large part of Maggie was more than suspicious of this sudden docility, but she chalked it up to pain and weariness. She located a raw steak without benefit of Kathleen's help, since the housekeeper was busy burning dinner, and carried it into the den. Rafe was sprawled bonelessly in his chair, his head back and eyes closed, and he *did* look both weary and as if he were in pain.

After a moment Maggie approached the chair from the back and very gently laid the steak over the injured eye. Rafe made no attempt to hold the steak in place himself, but sighed softly.

"Thank you, lass. That feels wonderful."

He did reach up then, but only to grasp her free hand where it rested on the back of the chair and hold it against his cheek.

"Did you really break your nose?"

Eyes still closed, he smiled crookedly. "Well, not thoroughly. A slight fracture. The first two times hurt a hell of a lot more."

"You've broken your nose three times?"

"Strictly speaking, someone else broke my nose

three times. Three someones. Four, actually, since two ganged up on me the first time."

"Has it occurred to you," she asked affably, "that fighting is not exactly a rational way to decide an argument?"

"It works," he pointed out.

She sighed. "Must be your Irish blood."

"Or just my combination of blood. The Apaches were no slouches as fighters, and neither were the Spaniards or the Mexicans. The Irish blood just makes me a little quicker off the mark."

It occurred to her then that this was the first time he hadn't stood when she came into a room, and that little lapse from his usual good manners made her soften even more toward him. She followed the line of thought, trying to ignore the feel of his cheek beneath her hand. "You have . . . old-fashioned manners. What part of your heritage is responsible for that?"

"A very recent heritage." He chuckled softly. "Mother. Dad brought her home after the war, a true Irish bride. She was small, with black hair and laughing dark eyes, and she made sure her boys were well-mannered. Drummed it into us, and I don't suppose any of us have forgotten even though it's been fifteen years. . . ."

Unconsciously she moved her hand against his face, sliding it down to stroke his jaw. She found it tense beneath her touch, and her throat ached because his voice had grown husky, grieving even after fifteen years. It was still husky when he spoke again.

"She always insisted we dress for dinner. We still do at Killara. At our mother's table."

Maggie's hand slipped downward to lie on his chest, and she bent without thought to rest her cheek against his. How old had he been when he'd lost his parents? Seventeen? She had been sixteen when she had, virtually if not in actuality, lost her father.

At least he'd had his brothers.

After a long moment Rafe said softly, "We never escape our pasts, do we, Maggie love? A distant past or a recent past . . . it's always with us."

"I don't know my . . . distant past," she said, equally soft, her cheek still pressed to his. "Only the recent one. I know I'm Irish, but I don't know if one of my ancestors married an Indian maiden or was buried at Boot Hill. I have no symbol claimed by an ancestor with a puckish sense of humor. I can't look at any land and know my family held it for generations, or dress for a meal at my mother's table. . . ."

As her wistful voice trailed away Rafe peeled the steak from his eye and tossed it aside. He grasped her wrist gently and drew her, unresisting, around the chair until he could pull her down across his lap. He held her lightly, his fingers toying with her ponytails until the elastic bands were gone and her hair spread across her back in a honey-colored curtain.

With incredible tenderness he said, "Poor lass, to be so alone. No wonder you want a ranch of your own so badly."

"My ranch," she whispered, the words coming without her volition. "Where I'll be in charge. Master of my fate. That's . . . so hard. But to be in control . . . to match the bloodlines of horses and—and *know* what traits you'll produce. Nothing left to chance." She released a sighing breath, dimly aware that the tables had turned. She had wanted to soothe his pain and grief, and now he was soothing what she had only just recognized as a wound of her own.

"You," she murmured, "you're like your horses. Pedigreed. Bloodlines you can trace back to your beginnings. What was it like, growing up a Delaney?" she asked, boneless beneath the stroking touch of his hand on her hair. "I've heard that you Delaneys are called the Shamrock Trinity. What was it like being the youngest of a trinity?"

Rafe was quiet for a minute. "It was . . . always having a sense of family, of roots. It was playing games in the old keep the family had brought over from Ireland and reassembled at Killara. It was reading the journals of ancestors and wondering if the present could ever live up to the past. It was . . . responsibility."

His voice lightened. "And it was a childhood. It was being punished—along with my brothers— because a clock was broken."

"A clock?"

"A very, very old clock. Made of bog wood dug up from the marshes of Ireland and hand carved with the Delaney shield. Old Shamus brought it over, and it ran perfectly. Until my brothers and I came along. It was broken, and never worked right again."

"Who did it?" she asked, curious.

He chuckled. "I didn't."

"None of you admitted it?"

"And so we were all three punished. A normal family story."

Maggie was silent for a moment, then she stirred slightly. "You're the youngest. Did that make a difference?"

"In growing up? No more than in any other family. There was a certain amount of competitiveness among us, but nothing unusual. We've always been close as brothers go—maybe because we're fairly close in age. Or maybe because there was never resentment over our places in the family business. Burke was always the brilliant one, the businessman. York was the renegade; mining and oil concerns suit him. And with me it was always horses."

She sat motionless, her head on his shoulder, listening to his deep, soft voice. She was tired and knew she was vulnerable, but the tales of Rafe's past behavior, and even the behavior she'd seen herself that seemed to confirm his reputation, was all fading from her thoughts. Could a heartbreaker be this gentle, this quiet and undemanding? Could a scalp-hunting charmer be perceptive enough to see and soothe her newly discovered pain at having no roots?

Funhouse mirrors: a man who was a dozen men. . . . It didn't make sense! Which was the true image?

Maggie was too tired to think about it. Sleepily she breathed in the musky scent of him, accepting what he was in this moment. She was only half aware of murmuring, "You're a very confusing man, boss," and felt more than heard him chuckle.

She never would have believed that she could fall asleep in his arms, but the last thing Maggie heard was a brief conversation that just barely reached her mind.

"Will you be wanting dinner, Mr. Rafe?"

"I don't think so, Kath. Thanks anyway."

"She was restless last night. Missing you, I'll be thinking."

"You would."

I didn't miss him, Maggie thought in drowsy mutiny.

"Mr. Rafe, the jeweler called today about the ring you dropped off to be cleaned. Would that be the one your dear mother meant for your bride?"

"Hush, Kath. Is it ready?"

"A few days, the man said."

"Good. That's good."

It was much later when Rafe carried a sleeping Maggie to her bed, and it took every shred of willpower he could command to lay her gently down and remove nothing but her shoes. He stood gazing at her for a moment, his heart lurching because her lovely face was so vulnerable in sleep, all her defenses down.

Lovely Maggie, he thought, as wary as a skittish colt when she was awake. But he could remember the touch of her hand earlier, a touch that had been seemingly instinctive and wholly willing. They had been closer in that moment—a shared interlude of remembered pain—than ever before.

A part of Rafe was willing to put his fate to the test right now, this minute. Wake her up with kisses, gambling on the response he'd felt from her more than once. But for all his recklessness Rafe had discovered a new emotion within himself these last days, born of his growing love for her: Caution. An almost desperate caution. If she had mattered less, he would have taken the chance of rushing her, giving in to the urges of his heart and his body.

She mattered too much.

Gazing at her sleeping face, he knew quite honestly and without conceit that she was the only thing he'd ever wanted that could be beyond his reach. Pride, wealth, power—none of it would win him Maggie's love.

He dared not move too quickly. In teasing her, he could—just—control his own desires. And it was worth the price of his restless nights to hear her laugh and to see the sparkle of baffled wrath in her eyes. To hear the little choked-off gurgle of laughter when she quite obviously wanted to yell furiously at him instead.

But Rafe didn't know how much longer he could continue as he had these last couple of weeks. That he had to continue was a certainty, because once he lost control, he would never again be able to pretend what he felt for her was a light or teasing emotion. And if Maggie realized that too soon, her own insecurities could drive her away before she could learn to feel anything for him.

All his life Rafe had been conscious of his own place in the history of his family. Bloodlines, she'd said. Maggie had no knowledge of hers, and that lack was something he knew she felt very deeply. She wanted a ranch of her own, a home to be master of. And he wasn't at all sure that she would be content with sharing *his* place. She'd worked so long and so hard, making a name for herself with nothing but her own skills and determination.

How he respected her for that! He himself had been born with a name made powerful by others, and though that had never seriously bothered him, he wondered now if he could have done as well as she if he'd started with nothing.

It was a sobering thought.

He had carved a niche for himself in the Delaney empire based on his own abilities and skills. But it had been *his* stock he'd handled, *his* land he'd walked upon. He had never been forced to work for others, to bow to another's wishes.

For the first time Rafe began to understand what had driven York to prove himself years before. York had felt an added incentive, of course. He had felt the need to prove himself a strong man, and not just a strong Delaney. But Rafe made a mental note not to try quite so hard to keep his restless brother close to home.

Home. . . .

Rafe turned and quietly left Maggie's room after a last glance. He had noticed her growing love for this land, and hoped he could convince her this was her home, the place where she belonged.

In the meantime he had no choice but to continue his teasing "seduction." Maggie mistrusted the rake, but rage at him though she inevitably did, laughter was never far from her voice or her eyes. And there was more than consolation, Rafe thought, in his patience.

He loved the sound of her laughter.

He hesitated outside the kitchen for a moment, listening to the clashes and rattles of Kathleen's "cleaning." His next step was risky, he knew. But Maggie's mood seemed definitely softened, and she just *might* accept his reasoning. Maybe. He fingered his nose gingerly and reflected with some satisfaction that his multicolored visage would rouse pity in the heart of a stone statue.

Maggie was hardly made of stone, and if he timed his explanation just right, he might get away with it. He stepped through the doorway of the kitchen, conjuring a disturbed expression.

"Kath? York needs you—"

* * *

Maggie opened her eyes in her own bedroom, fully awake in a jarring instant and conscious of several things. Sunlight filtering through her windows told her it was late morning; memory told her it was Sunday; and one glance told her that she'd slept in her clothes.

She could only vaguely recall a conversation between Rafe and Kathleen—something about a ring?—and had absolutely no memory of anything after that. He must have carried her to bed. Unnerved, Maggie climbed out of bed and stripped off her clothes.

Rafe had insisted some days before that she plan to take at least one full day off each week, and she had chosen Sunday since the ranch was usually quiet on that day. This day. Knowing she probably wouldn't ride today, she obeyed an impulse and dressed in a casual denim skirt with a red-checked blouse tied loosely at her waist.

Another impulse drove her to leave her hair loose, and she brushed it until it hung in a shining gold curtain to her waist.

Further unnerved by her own impulses, she left her bedroom and made her way through the quiet house. In the empty kitchen she fixed orange juice for herself and ate a slice of toast. Afterward she began wandering restlessly through the house. Where was Rafe? And Kathleen?

She walked down a narrow hallway that ran behind the kitchen along one wing. Her restlessness turned to interest when she realized she was in what was obviously the oldest part of the building. It was constructed of adobe, with small rooms and narrow windows. She hadn't stopped to think about it before, but this house had probably been rebuilt or at the very least added to, over the years as she'd been told had happened to Killara. Most of the rooms were for storage, filled with old furniture and various other antique items.

But one room captured her attention to the point of drawing her inside. It had obviously been a library or study at one time or another. Bookshelves lined two walls and contained dusty, old books, some clearly journals and notebooks. There were several very old maps framed and behind glass on the two remaining walls, and near the door was a row of shelves holding an amazing collection of steins ranging from a beaten—and somewhat battered—silver mug to a beautifully ornate porcelain stein that had probably never been sullied by beer.

"There you are," Rafe said, stepping into the room. "Thought I heard you in here."

For a moment Maggie was too busy staring at him to speak. Though the swelling had gone down in both his eye and nose, he still wore the hallmarks of a two-fisted free-for-all. If he'd been multicolored the day before, today he boasted glorious Technicolor.

"You look terrible!" she exclaimed without thinking, then corrected herself. To her, Rafe could never look terrible.

"Thank you," he said gravely.

"You look like you've been in a war."

"I feel like it." He winced as he took another step toward her. "I'm getting too old to use my body to turn a table into kindling."

"Did you?" she asked, startled.

He gave a low laugh. "It broke my fall. Somebody threw me."

Rather hastily she took his arm and led him to

an overstuffed leather armchair. "Sit down before you fall down."

"I'll live, lass." He sank into the chair, wincing again.

She stared down at him, and her curiosity shifted belatedly into gear. "I gather your brothers were in that fight as well?"

"Certainly. Delaneys always stand together—or fall together, as the case may be. I think I took the worst of it though. I usually do," he added philosophically.

"Don't you know how to duck?" Maggie demanded, half laughing.

Rafe looked mildly insulted. "Duck? As Burke constantly reminds me, fighting is a science. One does not *duck*. Bob and weave maybe, but never duck."

"You should have bobbed and weaved more then."

"When fists are coming at you from all directions, it's a bit difficult to know which way to weave."

She lifted a brow at him. "You know, it sounds as if you were in a barroom brawl." When his expression turned slightly sheepish, she choked back a laugh. "You were? Really?"

"My Irish blood," he murmured.

"In Hell's Bluff?" It was more statement than question, but Rafe nodded confirmation. Maggie was hardly gifted with second sight, but something about his expression prodded her to question further. "I thought it was a mining camp. There's a bar?"

He shifted a bit uncomfortably. "Of a sort."

"What's it called?"

He sighed. "The Soiled Dove."

She gazed at him for a long moment, then said bluntly. "Sounds like a cathouse."

Rafe seemed to have become fascinated by his scraped knuckles.

Maggie wanted to laugh. Or hit him with something. "You were in a brawl in a cathouse?"

"Don't leap to conclusions, please," he requested, pained.

"What conclusions could I possibly leap to? I'm just surprised that a Delaney has to pay, that's all." Her voice was terribly polite.

He stared pathetically at her. His fingers probed his nose. "Do I look as if I enjoyed myself?"

"Yes." Maggie was perfectly aware that it was ridiculous for her to play the part of enraged girlfriend—ridiculous and dangerous—but she was utterly fascinated by the picture of Rafe looking sheepish and uneasy.

"I was only there because I had to help York—"

"He needs help at his age?"

"That's not the kind of help I meant!" Rafe thrust fingers through his black hair and briefly gazed heavenward. "Look, the truth is, York needed help, so Burke and I went up there. We just *happened* to wind up in a brawl, and it just *happened* to take place where it did."

Maggie bit her tongue to hold back giggles. "That's a likely story," she managed to say, albeit a bit unsteadily.

"It's the truth!" he said, indignant.

She believed him. She didn't know why, but she believed him. And his injured expression finally cracked her control.

"You may well laugh," Rafe said, "but actually we were forced into the fight. Sort of."

"Forced? From what I've heard, you like to fight. You probably jumped at the chance to brawl!"

His black eyes gleamed at her. "Well, I'll admit I didn't hesitate. Fighting lets off steam, you know. And I've had a problem lately with . . . excess energy."

Deciding that her nerve wasn't quite up to probing *that* remark, Maggie turned quickly toward the shelves by the door. "These steins are fascinating. Did you collect them?"

Rafe laughed quietly behind her, but accepted the change of subject. "Yes, I did."

Stepping to the shelves, she picked up the heavy silver mug, and her finger traced its well-defined crease. "I bet they each have a story to tell. Right?"

"Right. York gave me that one. He came across it in Mexico."

She looked at Rafe, indicating the crease in the beaten silver. "This looks odd."

"Bullet. York was . . . uh, running for his life at the time. That mug saved him from a nasty wound."

Maggie blinked, then replaced the mug. "Oh. I see." She decided not to probe *that* either. She picked up the beautiful porcelain stein. "And this one?"

She thought she saw humor in his black eyes, but his expression was grave. "That one came from Burke. A German baroness gave it to him, hoping to remind him of a night they spent together. As you can see, he didn't want the reminder."

She replaced the stein on the shelf, not daring to ask about another. "You and your brothers certainly lead . . . interesting lives."

Rafe frowned a little, anxiety suddenly flickering

in his eyes. "Sometimes too interesting. Sometimes downright dangerous."

She looked at him searchingly. "Sometimes?"

He brooded, seemingly far away. "Sometimes," he murmured, "being a Delaney makes you a target."

Her heart lurched. "You—you're a target?"

He shrugged suddenly, as if he were casting off unwelcome thoughts. "Me? No. But Burke is at the moment." Then he went on, his voice casual, anxiety shuttered away in his eyes. "Anyway, only my brothers lead interesting lives. Mine's as dull as ditchwater."

"Uh-huh."

"The lady doubts my word, I see. Well, that's nothing new, is it?" He shifted in the chair, wincing slightly.

Maggie forgot about his past, and about the nebulous dangers of being a Delaney. She looked at him, at the wry expression and the dark eyes that had gone curiously bleak, and her heart turned over again. His light talk aside, he seemed both tired and defenseless, and nothing in her could stand against her concern for him.

"You should be lying down," she said.

"I was," he said, adding, "but I got lonely and came looking for you."

Maggie told her heart to stop lurching. "Well, you found me," she said as lightly as she could. "Why don't we move to the den? You can take the couch. By the way, where's Kathleen?"

Rafe had gotten to his feet, and now gazed at her with a comical wariness. "I'll tell you if you promise not to suspect my motives. I'm too tired and sore to fight today, lass."

"Where," she asked carefully, "is Kathleen?"

He sighed. "Hell's Bluff. York needed her, and I could hardly keep her from going, could I?"

She wanted to suspect his motives. She really did. But—dammit—he looked so vulnerable! Sighing, she murmured, "I see. I gather you don't know how long she'll be gone?"

"It depends on how long York needs her." Rafe was tentatively hopeful, presenting the absurd image of a spaniel in desperate need of a pat on the head.

Maggie resisted the urge to pat him. Leading the way to the den, she said over her shoulder, "I'll fix lunch, then. And dinner too."

"You don't have to, Maggie," he said, obviously uncomfortable. "Like I said, I didn't hire you to cook, and besides, it's your day off. We can make do today, and I'll get someone else in tomorrow—"

"Never mind. It's no bother, Rafe."

"If you're sure . . ."

They spent the day together. Maggie wanted to keep her guard up, some deeply buried instinct warning her that Rafe was far more dangerous in this vulnerable mood than in any other. But no matter how hard she tried, her voice refused to emerge briskly, and she couldn't bring herself to leave him alone.

They played Scrabble and watched an old movie on television. And they talked. As the afternoon wore on, she found herself relaxing completely in his company, even to the point of touching him casually and without thought. Touches that he accepted with a curiously endearing boyishness.

Occasional stray thoughts told Maggie that Rafe's humility coming hard on the heels of relentlessly seductive teasing was just a bit suspect. Just a bit. She ignored the thoughts.

And she ignored the alarm bells jangling in her every nerve when she and Rafe somehow wound up sitting close together on the couch. She was, she decided with detachment, certifiably out of her mind. There were, after all, certain things sane people avoided. Taunting bulls. Attack dogs. Hurricanes.

Vulnerable rakes.

Rafe drew her unresisting blody close. "Such a tiny lass," he murmured, his black eyes soft.

She watched her arms slip up around his neck with a vague sense of Great-oaks-from-little-acorns-grow. She should have run, she knew, when she'd had the chance.

His various injuries didn't seem to bother him as he feathered kisses along her jaw. He explored her face with a touch so light, she barely felt it, yet every sense came alive beneath his lips. She could feel her bones melting, feel the last shreds of willpower slipping away.

"So lovely," he whispered, his mouth just a breath away from hers. And then he was kissing her with a sudden urgent desire, branding her. It was more than a demand. It was a stark and primitive possession.

She felt heat sweep over her, and a dizzy weakness that drained away any thoughts of resistance. There was nothing teasing about his touch now, and she was as lost as she had known she would be. She couldn't have stopped him if saying no had been her ticket into heaven.

As it turned out, she didn't have to.

Her eyes opened, heavy-lidded and reluctant, when he finally raised his head. Boneless and quivering, she couldn't summon the will to do anything but stare helplessly at him.

He touched her face with a gentle hand, his black eyes burning. Then, even as she watched, the devil eyes began to dance wickedly. In a flashing instant he was somehow transformed from a vulnerable, yearning man into a triumphant rake.

"Who did you say could claim the superior cunning?" he murmured.

Six

For a full minute Maggie could only stare up at him. Her sluggish mind struggled with his question until she finally remembered the day in the tackroom and her method of getting away from him. She'd challenged him, she remembered him saying, because she'd claimed the superior cunning.

No Delaney could resist such a challenge.

Rage gave Maggie the careful control she needed to disentangle herself from his arms and get to her feet. She smoothed her clothing, giving the task her full attention for a moment, then finally looked at him. Looked at the sneaky, underhanded devil who had conned her so neatly that she'd forgotten the danger in him.

"You—"

"Don't say it," he interrupted, his eyes laughing

at her. "No lady would ever use the words I can see practically leaping from your tongue."

"Proud of yourself?" she asked shortly.

The laughter was extinguished from his gaze, and he looked up at her for a long moment before rising to his feet. His expression was more somber than she'd ever seen it before. "Not particularly."

The answer surprised her, and she didn't want to be surprised anymore by him. "Then why?" she demanded fiercely. "Just to make your damn point? Just to win? Because a Delaney can't bear to lose?" She rushed on before he could respond. "Well, you won! And I won't give you the satisfaction of hearing me lie about it!"

He caught her wrist when she would have turned away. "What did I win, Maggie?" he asked quietly.

She glared at him, furious with herself and more than enraged at him. He made her lose control of herself, and that apalled her in more ways than one. "You know what you won," she said, her voice shaking in spite of all her efforts. "We both know I wouldn't have—wouldn't have refused if—"

"If I'd carried you off to my bedroom?" His eyes held an expression she'd never seen before, something indefinable that caught the breath in her throat. "Yes, I knew that. But I didn't carry you to my bed, Maggie. I could have, but I didn't."

"You were making a point," she said hotly.

"Yes." His voice was very quiet. "But I think you missed the point, Maggie."

She wanted to fight the grip on her wrist, but it was a gentle yet inescapable hold. "I missed nothing!"

"Didn't you?" He sighed a bit raggedly. "A few minutes ago there was only one thing I wanted more than to make love to you."

She refused to ask, and he sighed again.

"Lass, the rake you think I am wouldn't have hesitated to carry you off to his bed in triumph. And, Lord knows, I want you badly enough to forget almost anything else. Except that. Except what you think I am. I can't forget that. And I was hoping . . ." He shook his head and released her wrist with a defeated shrug. "Well, I was obviously wrong, wasn't I?"

She rubbed her wrist absently, even though his grip had not hurt her. She stared at him, bewildered, wondering if this was just another role he'd assumed. "You . . . I don't know what you mean," she finally murmured, her rage, strangely enough, gone.

"I think you know, lass. If I wanted only another 'scalp,' we'd be in my bed right now." His mouth twisted oddly. "Self-denial isn't the trait of a rake. To be honest it isn't one of my strongest traits. There have been very few desires in my life that were beyond reach." He turned abruptly and wandered toward the fireplace, gazing down at the logs awaiting only a chilly night and a match. "Only one, in fact," he said in a low voice. "Only you."

She tore her gaze from his profile to stare down at the wrist she was still massaging, vaguely surprised that there were no marks of his hold on her skin. She could still feel his grip. And her heart was choking her because it was pounding in her throat. "That was what you proved," she managed to say. "I'm not . . . beyond reach. You could have . . . I wouldn't have said no."

"You wouldn't have said no," he agreed. He looked at her and his eyes held again that indefinable expression. "And in the morning—or before—you'd have been even further beyond my reach. I know that as certainly as I know my own name." He was silent for a moment, watching her, showing her yet another reflection of himself, an intense and brooding reflection she couldn't tear her gaze from. Then his mouth twisted in another painful smile.

"If I were a rake, Maggie, I would have snatched that opportunity to hold you in my arms for just a night. And in the morning, when you said goodbye, I would have promised you a glowing recommendation for your next training job—and we both know you'd have left. And I would always be a rake to you, and a bitter memory.

"But I'm not a rake, Maggie lass. My cursed reputation wasn't earned by a trail of fallen bodies and broken hearts. I have never in my life slept with a woman only to satisfy an appetite or chalk up another point on some imaginary scorecard." He sighed heavily. "And now I don't know what else I can say to you. Maybe I made the situation worse by playing the rake, but I'd hoped you'd realize how absurd it was. I won't say I didn't enjoy it. There's a bit of a rake in every man, I think, and your laughter was worth the price I paid for it."

"Price?" she whispered.

"Sleepless nights. And the fear that I'd push too hard, and you'd be gone."

Maggie knew her emotions were ragged and her thoughts confused. She tried to tell herself that this *was* just another role, another ploy. But the inescapable fact was that he could have carried her to his bed—and hadn't. She swallowed hard. "What do you want from me?"

He hesitated, then walked over to her, his eyes fathoms deep. "I want your trust, Maggie," he said huskily. "I want you to look past a reputation I didn't earn and *see* me. I want you to see the man I am, not the name I possess through an accident of birth, or the employer you work for."

"And then what?" She stared at him, aware of hot tears lodged somewhere in her throat, aware of a nameless fear.

His eyes searched hers. "And then . . . I hope you'll learn to love what you see."

She felt the tears burning, and refused to shed them. "It won't work, Rafe," she said flatly.

"Maggie, I—"

"It won't work. I'm sure you'd play King Cophetua with grace, but I'd make a lousy beggar-maid."

He gazed at the delicate face that was masklike in its stillness, and at the violet eyes that looked hot and shimmering. "Forget my name, Maggie," he said intensely. "We're two people, a man and a woman who feel something for each other. That's all that matters."

"Is it?" She laughed softly, the uneven sound a substitute for the tears. "No. You said it yourself: We can't escape our pasts. Or who we are. You're Rafe Delaney . . . and I work for you. What you own, I couldn't earn in a *lifetime*."

"What I own," he said, "was virtually handed to me, Maggie! Through an accident of birth, I was granted the kind of wealth and power that's vanishing these days because it took generations to build. I've built Shamrock into a name ranch, yes, and I've worked hard to do it. But I didn't start from nothing. If I had, we'd still be on unequal terms, you and I, because I wouldn't have gone a tenth the distance you have!"

She drew a shuddering breath. "Kind of you to say, but—"

"Kind, hell!" His voice was suddenly harsh. "It's the truth, Maggie. You've worked all your life, these last ten years alone, with the kind of strength and determination I doubt I could find in myself." His hands lifted, grasping her shoulders, his thumbs probing her collarbone. And his voice, when he went on, was suddenly gruff. "You amaze me, lass. You look as frail and delicate as a china doll, yet there's steel underneath. You handle animals and people with firmness and kindness and compassion, yet have a guard over yourself as if you're afraid to be touched. You've set your sights on a goal, and nothing is allowed to get in your way."

"Rafe—"

"Listen to me!" He took a deep breath. "It isn't wrong, what you've done. If I'd begun as you did, I like to think I'd have done the same. But goals change, Maggie. I'm asking you to think about that. There's no shame in turning from one goal to another. There's no lessening of yourself in becoming part of a team." The black eyes danced suddenly. "And we'd make a hell of a team, lass!"

Maggie allowed her heart to yearn for a moment—but just a moment. "And when it's over?" Her voice was toneless.

His hands tightened on her shoulders, and he laughed in a curiously self-mocking way. Something reckless stirred in his eyes. "You misunderstand, Maggie love. I'm asking you to be my wife."

She stared at him, her heart thudding violently against her ribs. Never in her wildest dreams had she imagined he'd want to marry her, and for an eternal moment she was utterly speechless. Then she stepped away from him with barely controlled violence, and his hands dropped. "That isn't funny!" she said fiercely.

"No," he agreed. He was smiling faintly, the crooked, reckless smile she had come to mistrust because it always seemed to herald some devilish move on his part. "Not funny. I've never been more serious in my life."

"Stop it!" She could feel panic sweep over her, emotions tangling until she couldn't think.

"I won't stop." The recklessness in his black eyes was joined by that other emotion she'd seen before, that not quite tame emotion. "I'll do whatever it takes to win you, Maggie. If it takes water dropping on a stone to wear away your resistance, then that's what I'll be. If it takes the rest of my life to get you to the altar, I'll consider it time well spent."

"You don't know what you're saying," she choked out.

"I know exactly what I'm saying."

She tried to think, but could only feel. The panic she felt came from years of being solitary, from the inner knowledge that her dream was attainable only if she fought for it alone and won it alone. Then the foundations of her life swayed and crumbled, battered by a new and devastating knowledge.

He saw her ambition so clearly, placing it unerringly at the very root of what she was. He knew her goal. And he was holding her goal in his hands, offering it to her. *And that was why she could never marry him.*

Because he would never be certain he was more important to her than the goal she'd attain by becoming his wife.

King Cophetua and the beggar-maid.

Maggie could feel her shoulders slump, and stiffened them with her last core of determination.

"I'll stay until you find another trainer," she said dully. "It shouldn't take long."

The crooked smile remained, but the expression in Rafe's eyes was grim. "That's your answer? Running away?"

She was too emotionally shell-shocked to be baited. In a childlike gesture of weariness she brushed the back of one hand over her forehead. "Sometimes it's the only answer. This time."

"No, Maggie. Not this time. You can't run far enough or fast enough to get away from me."

He seemed to be having trouble keeping his voice level, she thought vaguely, wondering at the jerky sound of it. She shook her head almost helplessly, staring up at him. "I told you. I won't play the beggar-maid. Leave it there, please, Rafe."

"Where's the woman who told me she was as good as any trainer twice her size? Where's the woman who *proved* that? You're no coward, Maggie! Why are you behaving like one?"

For the first time in her life Maggie could find none of the strength and pride that had brought her this far. She was defeated by something more powerful than anything she'd ever faced before, and it was within herself. "It looks like I am a coward," she murmured, almost to herself. "Maybe that's why it doesn't hurt to be called one."

"Maggie . . ." He framed her face with unsteady hands. "Doesn't it matter that I love you?"

Her heart stopped, then pounded painfully against her ribs. She looked at the man who would never again be a rake in her eyes, and she wanted to hold on to him with every muscle she possessed. But she stood still and silent, dragging the desperate longing into hiding somewhere deep within herself. She believed he loved her, although she couldn't believe it was a forever kind of love. There was nothing special about her, she was sure, to command that kind of affection.

He was special, and he did command that very special and lasting kind of emotion. She would love him until she died.

"Dammit, say something!" he ordered roughly. His instincts told him to kiss her still face and hold her tightly because she'd slipped away from him somehow, but a surer instinct warned that it would avail him nothing. They were both too near the ragged edge of their emotions, and he'd already discovered the danger of reckless impatience.

She stepped back from him carefully. "I'll go and start dinner." Her voice was calm and remote.

He clenched his jaw against the cry of protest rising in him, and his own voice was tight and strained. "All right." He waited until she reached the doorway, then spoke again. "Maggie?" She halted, but didn't turn. "You won't leave until I get another trainer?"

Her shoulders squared visibly. "No. No, I won't leave until you find someone else."

He stared at the doorway for a long time after she'd disappeared, then raked shaking fingers through his hair. "Damn," he said softly. "Damn . . . damn . . . *damn!*"

Moments later he was striding down the lane toward the barns, only vaguely aware of the deepening twilight and of the sounds of his employees closing up and calling it a night. Barns seven and eight were dark and still when he passed between them, the big, electrically powered doors closing off the halls and training rings and the security system turned on for the night. Main lights were going off in all the barns, and he reached number two just in time to prevent his foreman from closing it up.

"I'm taking Saladin out, Tom," he said, hearing the harsh rasp of his own voice. "I'll close up two when I get back."

After a single sharp glance that Rafe hardly noticed, Tom followed him into the still-lighted hall and watched his boss lead the chestnut from his stable. Tom studied Rafe's hands, which were steady and sure as Rafe groomed the stallion. Then Tom's gaze lifted and fixed on the face of the man he'd known for more than thirty years, and he felt something inside of him tighten.

He had thought he'd seen Rafe Delaney in every possible mood his volatile personality could boast. He had seen Rafe furious, reckless, grieving, proud, delighted, compassionate, brooding. He had seen him wade happily into various brawls, had seen him after a night or two spent in jail for "disturbing the peace." He had seen him shattered and silent after the deaths of his parents, and awed after the birth of a foal. He had watched Rafe struggle over the years to persuade his oldest brother to slow the hectic pace of his work, and to persuade his middle brother to remain close to home.

But Tom had never seen Rafe in this mood. He had never seen that face so still or those dark eyes so bleak. And he had never heard Rafe's voice as he'd heard it tonight.

Watching his employer and friend saddle the horse, Tom wished he could offer comfort, but knew better than to try. Since the deaths of his parents, Rafe had withdrawn from all but his brothers. He shut out no one intentionally, Tom knew, and his charm was such that no one who had not known him for thirty years would have felt the difference. But Tom did.

For all his charm Rafe Delaney was very much a loner. Being one third of a dynasty was more a burden than a blessing, and it kept him apart from most other men whether he willed it or not.

Tom wanted to stride up to the house and shake some sense into Maggie. He wanted to tell her things Rafe would never tell her, because Rafe was not self-centered enough to talk of such things. He wanted to tell her that some men would always be alone in a crowd, even if that crowd adored him. That some men could share *almost* all with much loved brothers . . . but only *all* with the woman they loved. That some men would walk through hell when they loved, and fight the devil for what they loved.

"I'll be back later," Rafe said.

Tom nodded and followed horse and rider from the wide hall. He watched until both disappeared up the lane and into the darkening night. He glanced toward the distant house, then stepped over to sit down on the narrow bench just inside the barn.

"Damn," he muttered.

Rafe allowed his horse time to loosen up at an easy pace, then they were racing over a narrow path at a gallop. Racing the wind. Daring the rising moon. Chasing the demons of the night.

Given his head and Rafe's hoarse encouragement, Saladin ran as his noble ancestors had run, head low and nostrils flaring, his delicate hooves flying over the ground in a mile-eating race.

Rafe didn't think. He let the horse run until he

slowed of his own volition, far from the compound, then guided Saladin to a high knoll and halted him. Then he simply waited. Waited for his heart to stop thudding. Waited for the stars to come close enough to drop into an open pocket. Waited for the raw beauty of the night to surround him. Waited for peace.

It came more slowly than ever before, but it did come.

He was able to think after a while, the unfamiliar blind despair seeping away slowly. And after a while, he stopped cursing his own recklessness in having pushed Maggie.

That was done and couldn't be undone.

He thought he knew why she had refused him. Instinct told him that she cared for him, was perhaps even beginning to love him. And his timing couldn't have been worse, he reflected. In trying to convince her he was no rake, he had incautiously become just the opposite, giving Maggie no time at all to adjust her perception of him.

And her confusion could have found voice in no other way. *Of course*, she refused to play the beggar-maid. Raw truth had echoed in her voice when she'd said, "What you own I couldn't earn in a lifetime." What she wanted most was his, and that was a wall between them. Maggie wouldn't marry to attain her goal.

Rafe watched the moon rise ever higher and thought long and hard. Defeat was not familiar to him, and he refused to admit himself beaten. He was, he knew, perfectly willing to do whatever it took to win Maggie's love; he simply could not envision a life without her. And, like Maggie, he had a strong tendency to focus on a goal and let nothing stand in his way.

He sat still in the saddle for a long time before turning Saladin back toward the compound. He spoke cheerfully to his foreman as he unsaddled and groomed the horse, then helped close up the barn and turn on the security system for the night. Then he strode toward the house.

Tom watched him walk up the lane and shook his head. Rafe's mercurial changes in mood were no puzzle to him after all these years, and he smothered a laugh as he headed toward his own cottage. Shamrock's newest trainer, Tom thought, had better watch her flanks, because the boss of Shamrock had decided on his strategy.

Rafe was not surprised to find the kitchen empty once he glanced at the clock and realized he'd been gone for hours. Maggie had left his dinner in the oven and had apparently retreated to her room. He enjoyed the meal and cleaned up after himself before going to his own room.

The next morning he found that she'd been up before him even though it was barely dawn, again leaving a meal ready for him. When he walked down the lane to the barns, the ranch's day had begun and his people were already busy. He went straight to barn four, halting just as he reached it to observe a large van driving up the lane from the main road.

He was surprised they'd arrived so early, and when the van stopped, he had a brief word with the driver. Then he went into Maggie's barn.

She was at the far end of the hall, leaning against the gate to the training ring and watching three young Saddlebreds being worked. As he neared her Rafe saw that she was pale and looked tired, and he fought the instincts urging him to take her in his arms. Instead, he moved silently behind her and dropped a quick kiss on the nape of her neck left bare by her two ponytails. He was smiling easily when she swung around to face him.

"Good morning," he said. "We've got a new horse outside. How about helping me unload him?"

There was color in Maggie's face now, and she seemed confused. "Oh—of course," she murmured. She started down the hall. "Another horse for me—for this barn?" she corrected herself hurriedly.

"Another horse for you." He ignored the glance she shot him.

"Rafe, I'm—"

"This is a special horse," he interrupted calmly, "and I'm expecting great things of him. He came highly recommended." Rafe chuckled quietly as they came out into the brightening day. "He's the only horse on Shamrock insured through Lloyd's of London."

She looked at him, bewildered, then shrugged and headed for the side door of the dark-colored van. She saw no logo or other identifying mark on the vehicle, and wondered where this horse had been purchased. The driver was standing to one side talking quietly to Rafe, so she let down the ramp herself and entered the van. And even though the single occupant of the van was blanketed from just behind his ears to his tail, his entire body covered, she knew where the horse had come from.

She touched the perfect white exclamation point between flaring nostrils, unsurprised to see her hand was trembling. This was a horse that a trainer or owner could well wait a lifetime for and never encounter, a horse with utterly perfect conformation, pure bloodlines, incredible beauty and performance, and a temperament that made working with him a joy.

He stood over sixteen hands tall at the withers with the pads on his front hooves and was powerfully muscled even though barely four years old. He was a three-time Walking Horse National Champion: Warlock.

Maggie carefully untied the stallion and led him from the van, taking care going down the ramp. When they stood outside, Warlock lifted his head high and called a commanding challenge to any other stallion within earshot, yet he was instantly obedient to Maggie's hand on the lead rope. She was only vaguely aware of the van pulling away, and of the gathering crowd of admiring Shamrock people.

"Let's have a look at him," Rafe said. He stepped to the horse's side and unfastened the blanket, folding it neatly as he removed it to reveal Warlock in all his ebony beauty.

"Rafe . . ." Maggie stared up at the man at her side, forgetting, for a moment, what had passed between them yesterday. "Hawkes wouldn't sell him; he just laughed at the offers!"

"He didn't laugh at my offer." Rafe smiled down at her. "We'd better take him inside, don't you think? He isn't used to this Arizona sun."

Maggie came to herself with a start, and quickly led the stallion inside the cool barn hall. In her elation she forgot everything, feeling the excitement only another trainer could know. Warlock! To be able to ride and show such a horse! To watch his foals as they matured, searching for the sire's wonderful traits in his offspring.

A once in a lifetime opportunity!

She turned the stallion into one of the four specially reinforced stables meant to house the more powerful and erratic males, then leaned over the Dutch door to watch him acquaint himself with his new home. "He's beautiful," she murmured.

"That he is." Rafe was standing beside her, watching also. "We'll have to find brood mares worthy of him, lass. The only real champion mare we have on the place now is your Calypso, I'd say. Do you plan to show her another season, or breed her?"

The tacit offer brought Maggie's gaze to his face, and for a moment she allowed herself to dream. Calypso and Warlock—what a foal they'd produce! But then she remembered everything, and she turned back to stare at the horse of her dreams. "I . . . couldn't afford the stud fee," she said in the steadiest voice she could command.

"No fee," Rafe said casually. "You earned a foal just by recommending him, Maggie. Call it a bonus, if you like."

It was a not-unheard-of offer from an owner to a trainer, but the ramifications of his words shocked her. "You—you bought him on my say-so?" She knew he hadn't left the ranch to fly East since her arrival. "You didn't even go *see* him first?"

"No need to. You said he was the best."

"Yes, but . . . Rafe, that was my opinion! What if I'm wrong?" She was shaken, knowing that he must have paid the earth for Warlock only on her word that the horse was worth the price.

He looked down at her for a moment, his dark eyes very intent and utterly serious. "You know horses, Maggie. You've lived with them, ridden them, trained them, shown them. You've devoted your life to horses. I trust your opinion as I'd trust my own."

She swallowed hard. There was simple truth in his eyes and his low voice, and she didn't doubt his sincerity. Never in her life had she been so trusted. Looking away blindly, she whispered, "Thank you."

"You don't value yourself enough." His hand was warm on her cheek as he gently forced her to meet his eyes again. "And don't thank me for the truth." He sighed. "What a team you and I would make. Maggie—"

"I'm leaving, Rafe." It took all her willpower to force the words out, to say what left her torn inside. "As soon as you find another trainer."

After a moment he nodded. "I see. No second thoughts in the quiet hours of the night?"

"No."

"Well, I can hardly lock you in a turret, can I?" He smiled oddly. "More's the pity. Those days are past—even for a Delaney accustomed to riding roughshod over people."

"I never said that," she protested almost inaudibly.

"No, you never said that," he agreed dryly. "You said a few other idiotic things, but not that."

"I didn't—"

"Oh, yes, you did." His voice, which had been calm and level, took on a suddenly intense tone. "Tell me something, lass. Do you think one person has the right to sacrifice another person's happiness?"

"No, of course not."

"Then why are you prepared to do just that?" he demanded softly.

She stared at him.

He went on, his gaze holding hers. "You think if you married me, I'd never be sure it was me more than the ranch you wanted. That's it, isn't it, Maggie? I don't know if you love me, but I know that's the reason you won't marry me. I've got what you've worked for all your life, and *that's* what's standing between us."

Maggie wanted to pull away, but the stable door was at her back, and there was no way of resisting Rafe's formidable strength. She didn't want to get into this, didn't want her decision challenged in this dangerous way. "Rafe, don't, please . . ."

"I won't, Maggie," he said very quietly. "I won't let you sacrifice my happiness because of some damn stupid scruple! You've said you're leaving; I can't keep you here against your will. But you'll stay until I find another trainer, and I'll do everything in my power to convince you to marry me. You may leave me, but I'll make damned sure you never forget me!"

He pulled her against him roughly, holding her so tightly that she could feel the muscled power of his body branding her own. And the lips that captured hers were hot and hard with a need that made the blood roar in her ears. He kissed her as if it were the last chance he'd ever have, and Maggie was trembling violently when, moments later, he abruptly released her and strode away.

Seven

From the moment Rafe walked away from her, Maggie knew that she should leave immediately. For some reason she couldn't fathom, he'd decided she was what he wanted, and though he obviously didn't intend to keep her on the ranch against her will, neither had he accepted her rejection.

Her willpower was shaky where he was concerned, and Maggie was very afraid that she'd give in to him because she loved him, without counting the cost. Away from him she could understand rationally that if she married him, Rafe could never be sure of her motives. Near him she had to fight the urge to ignore what he so generously called a "damn stupid scruple" and fling herself into his arms, into his keeping.

But it was more than a scruple. She could be certain herself, deep in her heart, that Shamrock meant nothing to her compared to Rafe. She could have no doubt whatsoever that if Rafe had nothing, she would gladly have walked by his side throughout their lives. But Rafe could never be certain of that. And even if the question never disturbed him, she would always carry the burden of it on her own shoulders.

She was almost willing to risk it. Almost willing to believe in Rafe's love and put aside the question of her motives . . . for a while. Because she couldn't help but believe that it would only be for a while, that Rafe would sooner or later find his love for her less than he had believed it to be.

And then what? He'd have a wife he didn't love and couldn't entirely trust. She doubted his family took divorce lightly. Would he end his marriage in court, or choose to live with his mistake whatever the cost?

Maggie knew that she was anticipating problems. She knew that she was raising every wall she could think of between them. But she had no choice. It was the only way she knew to find the strength she'd need to leave him.

For a few days Maggie was able to lose herself in her work. There was a great deal of attention focused on her because of Warlock. When she worked him in the training ring, there was always a crowd, and she often answered questions from the other trainers about methods used to prepare gaited horses for the show ring.

As for Rafe, she found that he could display yet another facet of his personality, yet another mirror image of a single man. He remained nearby, as he had in past weeks, but he was quieter and far less effusive than the "rake" who had so relentlessly pursued her. He was still inclined to pick her up and place her in a saddle, still quick to hug her or drop an unexpected kiss on the nape of her neck, but he no longer chose to carry on his "flirtation" beneath the eyes of the other Shamrock people.

It was a kind of pressure Maggie felt keenly, yet couldn't, for some reason, protest. Whenever an objection rose in her throat, she would find his gaze on her and, breathless, would forget the words.

They were rarely alone and didn't talk when they were. Very quietly Rafe had hired a temporary housekeeper until Kathleen's return, a brisk and capable woman who cooked and cleaned and showed no inclination for the familiar talk that had been the Irish housekeeper's saving grace.

Maggie felt lonely as never before in her life.

She dreaded the inevitable moment of her leaving, working as hard as she'd ever done to continue the training of her people and horses. That another trainer had not instantly been summoned didn't surprise her. Rafe had hired her only after weeks of searching, and he'd hardly pick another trainer with less care. But her tension grew with the long working days and sleepless nights, until she knew she was on the brink of some reckless action, every bit as incautious as Rafe at his worst.

By Wednesday afternoon Rafe had either guessed her nervy state or else it had become painfully obvious.

"How long can we go on this way?" he asked her quietly.

Maggie had just turned Warlock into his stable, and she concentrated on fastening the door rather than looking at Rafe. "Have you found another trainer?"

"No. Now answer my question."

She clipped the lead rope to a ring fastened near the door and finally turned to gaze at Rafe. They were alone in the cool hall. "What do you want me to say, Rafe? It's . . . already been said."

He drew in a deep breath and straightened away from the wall, staring at her. "I don't think so. I've never yet seen a problem that couldn't be solved in some way. And I happen to believe that you and I belong together. What I *don't* believe is that you'd marry me to get this ranch. So where's our problem, Maggie? Tell me that."

She squared her shoulders and met his gaze as steadily as she could, realizing that he wouldn't be put off this time. "Which problem, Rafe? Do you want a list? All right, then. You have what I want, what I've worked for all these years—"

"You wouldn't marry me for the ranch," he said flatly.

She ignored the interruption. "You're a Delaney, and no matter what you say, that *means* something in this country. It means wealth and power and a heritage that makes you a part of a dynasty. And I'm a woman who trains horses, a woman who has little more than I can carry in a Jeep, a woman with no background, no understanding of what it means to be who you are. What would your brothers say if you married your trainer, Rafe?"

"They'd congratulate me on my lovely bride," he said very softly. "For Pete's sake, Maggie, we don't live in the Middle Ages! And the Delaneys aren't royalty! Old Shamus was a reiver and a smuggler; William is buried on Boot Hill—and countless others of my ancestors were as wild as bedamned!"

"But you know who they were." Her voice was little more than a whisper. "You know where you came from and where you belong."

He stepped forward abruptly and caught her hand. "Maggie," he said gently, "my mother was a housemaid in Ireland when Dad found her. An orphan with no family and no money. She became a Delaney; she wasn't born to it. But no one was prouder of our family than she was. And when Rising Star married Joshua, she accepted a way of life that was totally different from all that she knew—and became a Delaney."

He stared down at Maggie, his dark eyes intense. "Maggie love, think of those two women. One an Apache woman who lived in a time of violent unrest, and the other an Irish housemaid who had survived a brutal war. Their men loved them for what they were, not for what they could bring materially to the family. They were women to walk beside a man and build a life with him. They took the Delaney name—and enriched it.

"Think about them, Maggie. And think of yourself. You don't know it, but you're an amazing woman. And together you and I could make this ranch mean more than either of us ever dreamed. I could never do it alone, lass."

"You could—"

"No. I know horses and I know business, but I can't tame a devil-horse in a single afternoon, or ride a gaited horse into the show ring. And I can't work to build this ranch when there's no one to share it with me. Not now. Not when I've discovered what sharing could mean." His voice was low and filled with feeling. "I've . . . missed the sound of your laugh, Maggie. And the sparkle in your lovely eyes when you're enraged at me. This place would be empty for me if you left."

Maggie swallowed hard. Her mind was whirling, her heart aching with . . . possibilities. She loved this man so much, yet a lifetime of harsh reality told her that he could never love someone like her. And from somewhere, from some almost dry well of strength, she produced a faint smile. "You're saying all the things I need to hear," she said lightly.

He swore softly. "Is that why you think I've been talking? Just making pretty speeches? Maggie, I love you! And there's only one thing you could say to convince me we don't have a future together." His free hand lifted her chin, forcing her to meet his eyes. "Tell me you don't love me, that there's no chance you could learn to love me. Tell me that, Maggie."

Her eyes skittered away from his, the words he'd asked for stuck somewhere in her throat. She couldn't say it. Couldn't lie about her feelings. It took every ounce of willpower she could summon to keep from shouting out her love and flinging her arms around his neck.

But in not saying she didn't love him, she was telling him that she did.

The hand at her chin seemed unsteady as Rafe said roughly, "I'm going to marry you, lass." The devil-black eyes abruptly began to laugh and his crooked smile dawned. "What's more, I've decided the days of locking unwilling maidens in turrets aren't *that* far in the past. Although the closest thing to a turret I can offer is the old Norman keep at Killara. . . ."

For the first time in days, Maggie found herself torn between laughter and anger, and it was a good feeling. He was acting rakish again, and she knew she had a definite soft spot for this particular rake. Besides, he couldn't be serious. Could he? Backing away a step, she said carefully, "If I thought you were serious, I'd catch the first mule train out of here."

Still smiling, Rafe winked at her and turned to stroll away. Whistling something, she decided, about Irish eyes.

She started slightly when Warlock nudged her over the door, and turned to frown at him. "Kipling was wrong," she told the stallion uneasily. "The male of the species is far more deadly than the female. And I wish I knew what *that* male was up to!"

Well, she knew the answer, of course. Basically. And a reckless excitement began building within her. She had talked herself out of marrying Rafe, argued with him and with herself, worked herself almost to exhaustion, and spent too many wakeful nights. She had erected every possible wall between them and considered problems that might well never occur.

What she had not done, until this moment, was simply listen to her own heart and the instincts that had never yet proved false. She loved Rafe Delaney, and he seemed certain of his own love for her. Why was she so intent on fighting that? Why not simply accept the incredible smile of fate?

Maggie smiled herself and patted Warlock on his curiously marked nose.

Maggie sat bolt upright in bed, disoriented and afraid. The loud alarm ringing through the house jarred her down to her bones. For an eternal moment she didn't know what was going on, her mind sluggishly reminding her that she'd gone to her room immediately after dinner because she'd felt unusually shy in Rafe's presence. Then some instinct told her that either the ranch's security system had been breached or—the thought stopped the breath in her throat—there was a fire.

Throwing off the covers, she dressed with desperate haste, cursing because she couldn't see the barns from this side of the house. It was almost dawn but still dark outside, and as she rushed from her room and down the dimly lit hallway Maggie remembered the horror she had witnessed only once in her life: a burning barn with screaming horses trapped inside.

She met Rafe as he was about to enter the kitchen, taking the quickest route outside. He had obviously dressed in haste but was, like her, fully dressed and wide-awake. And his face was grim.

"Rafe?"

"It's fire." He led the way through the kitchen, pausing only to grab a handful of dishtowels from a drawer before heading out the back door. "Number four, Maggie."

She felt her heart catch as she raced beside him down the lane. She could hear the shrieks of frightened horses and within moments was able to see barn four silhouetted against the gray sky, its entire roof in flames. Shouts rose above the roar of the fire as Shamrock people arrived at the barn, some in vehicles and some on foot.

"Rafe, the sprinkler system's out!" Tom had appeared beside them almost magically, his lined face older than Maggie had ever seen it. "The whole damn compound is without water or power!"

The boss of Shamrock didn't waste time with questions. "Get the portable pump and run it straight into the tanks. Run as many hoses as you can. Wet down barns three and five so they won't catch."

"The horses!" Maggie yelled, starting forward only to halt as Rafe grabbed her arm.

"Wait, lass. With the power out, all the doors are jammed—even the paddock doors. We'll have to break through to get the horses out." He dumped the dishcloths into her arms and reached for the ax one of the men was holding out to him, then ran for the main door of the barn.

Maggie was close behind, feeling helpless as she watched Rafe and the other man attack the huge door with fierce blows. The heat was building, coming at them in waves, the bales of hay within the loft feeding the fire's hungry need. She knew they had very little time to get the horses out before the loft would cave in on the helpless, trapped animals below.

She found Russell and Mike beside her, and handed each of them a couple of the cloths she was still holding, keeping two herself and dumping the rest on the ground. She and her two apprentices, she knew, would stand a better chance of getting the terrified animals out of the barn since they were accustomed to handling these particular horses.

Remembering that other burning barn that still flamed in her nightmares, Maggie prayed silently as she waited for a large enough opening to fit herself through. Prayed that the animals would be controllable in their terror. Prayed that the loft would hold until a dozen horses could be saved.

And she wondered, fleetingly, what could have caused the fire. Since the power was out all over the compound, it seemed reasonable that some electrical malfunction could prove to be the culprit.

But a niggling certainty told her that was next to impossible. She had been on countless ranches and worked in many stables, and none had possessed a security system with as many safety checks as Shamrock's. Each barn was individually protected by an independent security and fire system; the sprinklers were tied into the underground tanks holding water for the ranch and the waterlines were kept pressurized.

How could the entire compound have been rendered powerless and without water? And why had the fire alarm worked when nothing else did?

The questions vanished from her mind as a ragged opening was carved in the big door, and Maggie slipped instantly through before Rafe could stop her.

"Maggie!"

She coughed as heavy smoke filled her lungs and brought tears to her eyes, but her steps took her automatically to the nearest stall. Some flaming bits of hay were spilling down from the loft and into the wide hall, and it was an eerie and awful feeling to find her way to the stall by the reddish, flickering light of hungry flames. Some of the horses were trying to kick their doors down, while others frantically circled the traps of their stables and screamed in terror.

A violent nudge nearly knocked her down, and Maggie found Figure at her side. His long ears were pinned flat, the rheumy eyes watering from the smoke, and she could see the burro had been trying in vain to open the stable door. Diablo's stable, she realized instantly. Scars in the wood all around the bolt testified to Figure's desperation—and testified to the strength of bolts made specifically to foil any animal's attempt to unfasten them.

Pushing the anxious burro to one side, Maggie reached for the lead rope hanging on the wall, then unbolted the stable door and flung it open. She knew the horse was Diablo only because she knew it was his stall. The dim and ugly red glow provided very little light and tears were streaming from her eyes because of the smoke. She crooned softly as the stallion snorted and sidled away from her, holding on to her patience because she knew it was her only hope. Diablo trembled, jerking away from her twice before she was finally able to get the cloths fastened to his halter and covering his eyes. He was too terrified by the fire even to be calmed by Figure's presence. But with his eyes covered, he was instantly, almost magically quieted, and she was able to lead him quickly from his stall.

Russel and Mike hurried past her as she neared the door, the opening now just barely large enough for a horse to fit through. She pulled the stallion outside and into the clear as Figure followed, only vaguely aware that it had grown lighter during the minutes she'd been inside the barn.

Coughing violently, she handed the lead rope to Lisa. "Take him to one of the other barns," she said, gasping, "and put him in a paddock. Let Figure stay with him to keep him calm. The mares can go in the corral, but the stallions would kill each other. We'll have to keep them separated." She bent to get another cloth from the ground as Lisa led the blindfolded horse down the lane with the burro at their heels.

Rafe grabbed her arm, his free hand holding a blindfolded mare he'd just led out. "You aren't going back in there!" He thrust the lead rope into her hand and took the cloth from her. "Get her to the corral, Maggie."

He dived back through the opening before she could object, and she quickly led the mare across the lane to the large corral. She tore the blindfold off and released the horse safely within the fence, then raced back to the barn, mentally counting as she watched Russell lead her own Dust Devil from the barn. Three. Three safe. Nine horses to go. . . .

"Take him to a paddock, Russ!" she shouted. The roar of the fire was louder now, like some hungry beast demanding to be fed. Three men held hoses spraying water on the barn, but she could see that it would never be enough. By the grace of God there was no wind, so the other barns appeared to be safe, but number four, she knew, would burn to the ground.

She thought she heard a helicopter, but paid little attention to the sound. She took another mare from Mike just outside the door and headed to the corral with her as he disappeared back into the barn.

Four. Four now. Eight to go.

Rafe came out later with a stallion, and she paused a moment after he handed her the lead-rope. "Rafe, your lungs can't take all that smoke—" He was coughing violently.

He grabbed a cloth from her and turned back to the opening nearly hidden by thick smoke. "Get him out of here, Maggie!"

Swearing unsteadily, she quickly led the stallion down the lane to one of the other barns and released him into a paddock. She had just started back down the lane at a run when a shout reached her and she half turned in automatic response.

"Where's Rafe?"

In spite of her fear and anxiety Maggie was a woman—and no woman made of anything other than stone could have failed to react as she reacted. It was past dawn now, and she could see the stranger's face clearly. It was a face utterly beautiful in its masculine perfection, a heart-stopping, mind-boggling face—and her mind boggled. For an eternal instant she could only stare at him in astonishment. He had thick, wavy black hair and clear blue eyes, and not even his grimly set expression could detract from his beauty.

"Where's Rafe?" he repeated impatiently, either uncaring or accustomed to mindless stares from women.

Maggie came to herself with a start. "In the barn," she answered, heading back down the lane quickly with the stranger racing beside her. She didn't know who he was and didn't particularly care once the shock of him had worn off. Her entire attention was focused on the raging inferno that was a death trap for men and horses.

They reached the door just as Rafe handed over another mare to waiting hands. His face was white beneath the soot and grime, his eyes red-rimmed and watering, and he was coughing so hard, he could barely stand.

The stranger with Maggie grabbed the cloth from Rafe's hand and snapped at her, "Keep him out here!"

"How the hell am I supposed to do that?" she snapped right back. "He's bigger than I am!"

"I'll knock him down," the stranger growled, "and you can sit on him!"

But he plunged toward the barn with no more than a glare toward Rafe.

"York!" Rafe would have dived right back into the barn, but Maggie put both hands against his chest and shoved him away as the stranger disappeared through the door.

"Rafe, you can't go back in there!"

"Neither can York, dammit!"

Maggie knew who the stranger was now, and a detached part of her mind thought what a wonderful way she'd chosen to meet Rafe's brother. First she'd stared at him like a moron, then she'd yelled at him. Wonderful.

She forced Rafe to back away, aided by the fact that he was coughing too hard to struggle very much. "York can take care of himself," she said. "And if you go back in there, he'll have to carry you out!" She glanced across the lane at the corral, quickly counting. Eight horses were now safe; four to go. She thought she saw someone moving within the corral, but assumed one of the hands was simply remaining there to soothe the terrified horses, and dismissed the matter from her mind.

The sun was rising, adding its orange glow to the hellish scene surrounding barn four. The flaming barn was still silhouetted against the sky, and ominous groaning and cracking sounds now came from within. Maggie could see the men still battling with hoses, and there were other men working to smother the sparks jumping from the building and onto the dry patches of grass nearby.

Horses were still screaming in fright, and those in barns three and five were close enough to be panicked by the smoke and the fury of sound all around them.

Maggie counted again. Three to go.

York emerged with a mare, and someone else pushed past him to vanish into the smoking hell. He paused, coughing, then directed a quick question at Rafe.

"Burke here?"

Rafe gestured toward the other end of the barn, where another tall, dark-haired man was helping battle the fire. "Got here a few minutes ago. York, stay the hell out of there!" He grabbed his brother's arm.

"There are a couple more horses—"

"And at least three of my people are in there getting them out," Rafe interrupted roughly, pulling his brother away from the burning barn.

Maggie was dimly aware that time had somehow slowed, aware that less than an hour had passed since the alarm had awakened them so violently. In spite of the hurried movements around her, she had the eerie sensation of dragging time. Even her heart seemed to be pounding in an altered, slower rhythm.

And the sound she heard then, a peculiar echoing *cra-aack*, puzzled her momentarily. It came from behind them, she realized, from the corral, and there was something familiar about the sound.

"Down!" York snapped, then he was bending low and running toward the other end of the barn, where men were diving for the ground.

Rafe paused only to push Maggie to the ground with a hurried command to stay there before following his brother in a crouching run.

She knew, then, and astonishment washed over her. Who would be shooting at them? Good Lord! Something right out of the movies! It didn't happen in real life, Maggie tried to tell herself—except that it was happening.

Whoever it was was shooting steadily, forcing everyone to take cover or at least lie flat on the ground, and two of the Delaney brothers were racing toward the third—who, Maggie realized in horror, was the gunman's target. Her heart clenched in fear, then lurched sickeningly when one of the tall, dark-haired men stumbled and fell, and she was up in an instant to race forward.

Through the smoke and shimmering heat of the blazing barn, it was almost impossible to tell which brother had been shot, and Maggie was nearly crazy with the fear that it was Rafe. Someone had found a rifle in one of the trucks and was returning the fire, either deliberately or accidently shooting wide. Maggie hoped that it was the former, since there were horses in that corral, but she hardly wasted a thought on the question.

She found the three Delaneys sheltered from the gunfire behind a parked truck, and was jerked down by Rafe instantly.

"Dammit, Maggie, I told you to stay down!" He didn't waste further breath raging at her, since he was somewhat occupied in tying a ragged bandage torn from his shirt around York's upper left arm.

Maggie told her heart to quit pounding since all the brothers were reasonably safe. York's wound seemed to be fairly minor. He was leaning against the truck while Rafe worked on his arm and seemed apparently more disgusted than hurt at his wound. He was also swearing steadily in a low voice and being admirably creative about it. She listened with a fascination born out of shock and near-hysteria. He hadn't, she thought with respect, repeated himself once.

Realizing that the giggle in her throat was perfectly natural under the circumstances, Maggie nonetheless dragged her attention from York's colorful curses and concentrated on Rafe's savage voice.

"Will you take the damned threats seriously *now*?" he demanded of his eldest brother. "Hell, I wondered why the whole system was out of commission. Now we know!"

"Now we know." Burke Delaney's voice was level, his striking green eyes filled with icy anger as he glanced in the direction of the sniper.

Maggie studied this brother's face with utter captivation, a very sane and logical part of her mind telling her that she'd better concentrate on something—anything—or else she'd fly into a million pieces.

Burke seemed as good a focus as any.

The oldest Delaney brother was a bit more rugged than the other two, a tough man with more than a hint of ruthlessness in his strong face. That might of course, Maggie decided fairly, be due to their present circumstances, but she didn't think so.

Apart, any one of the brothers would have looked formidable. Together, they literally shouted a kind of raw strength and power that was rare in these reasonably civilized times. Maggie was enchanted by them, her gaze moving from one to the other wonderingly. She no longer heard gunfire, and blinked in surprise when a hand waved suddenly in front of her face.

"Maggie?"

She looked at Rafe and smiled. "I'm fine," she said brightly. She sat, perfectly calm, with her legs folded and her hands lying placidly in her lap, and wondered why he was looking at her so strangely.

Rafe seemed to be fighting a grin. "Are you?" He glanced at his brothers, both of whom were also gazing at Maggie. "Shamrock's newest trainer, Maggie O'Riley," he said.

Before he could offer to introduce the brothers, she nodded at them cheerfully. "And you're the other two Delaneys. I yelled at York, and Burke's the mean-looking one." She blinked and rubbed her forehead fretfully. "I didn't say that," she murmured.

"She's had a rough morning," Rafe explained to his laughing brothers, chuckling himself.

"Well, she *did* yell at me," York said gravely. "And Burke *does* look mean. It must be the light or something, but he definitely looks mean."

Seemingly amused, Burke said dryly, "I've been called worse."

"Haven't we all?" York sighed, then winced as he apparently disturbed his wounded arm. "Hell. Has that bastard stopped shooting?"

Rafe peered cautiously around the truck's bumper. "From the looks of it, yes. I can see Tom over by the corral, and a couple of others. The sniper must have run for the river."

"There's no way we'll catch him now," Burke said decisively, then added in a hard voice, "but he won't get away for good."

Maggie watched, still suspended in that peculiar fascination, while Rafe got up, and he and Burke helped York to his feet.

"Come on, brother," he said. "Let's get you to the vet."

"The *what*?"

"Sorry. Only doctor on the place, I'm afraid."

"Oh, great! That's two I owe you, little brother," York said meaningfully.

"Two? What do you—" Rafe broke off abruptly, looking as if he wished he'd kept his mouth shut.

"Kathleen," York said in a very gentle voice.

It was Rafe's turn to wince. "Why don't we talk about that later," he suggested.

"We will," York said, amiable now. "I want the use of both arms when we talk about that."

"Don't quarrel, kids," Burke said. "We still have a burning barn to deal with."

Maggie rose to her feet, watching the two unhurt brothers flanking the wounded one as they walked over to where Dr. Woods was treating a few minor injuries from the back of his well-equipped pickup truck. She frowned a little, counting carefully in her mind, but not quite certain what she was counting. Except that the number she came up with was eleven, and that was wrong somehow. Then Russell appeared at her side, gasping for breath, his grimy face exhausted.

"Maggie . . . we tried . . . but he knocked Lisa down . . . and I had to get her out of there. . . . The loft's about to go. . . ."

Icy fear and horror yanked Maggie back from the edge of hysteria, and she stared at him. "My God," she whispered. "Twelve. It should have been twelve!" And she raced toward the flaming pyre that still held a horse trapped.

"Maggie!"

Rafe heard the shout and turned instantly, his eyes finding her running form silhouetted against the burning barn. And then he saw Russell's ashen face, and heard him shout words that stopped his heart.

"Rafe, she's going in after Warlock!"

With a harsh sound Rafe broke the sudden grip of Burke's hand and whirled back to the barn. He could see that the loft was already caving in, beams falling with groaning crashes inside, and he knew with a horrible certainty that Maggie would never make it out of there alive.

He ran.

Eight

Rafe nearly hit his brother when Burke stopped him just short of the ragged opening in the barn door, and probably would have except that he found his arms suddenly tangled in the soaking weight of a horse blanket. He realized without thought that someone had managed to get some of the tack and equipment out, and that Burke had hurriedly wet down one of the blankets. Two blankets, he thought dimly as he saw his brother drape one around his own shoulders.

"Keep it over your head," Burke ordered tersely. "And for God's sake watch out for falling beams!"

A part of Rafe's mind told him that Burke had no business going into the burning barn, but he didn't waste time arguing when he knew he'd lose. Pulling the dripping blanket around him, he lurched through the opening—and into Purgatory.

This end of the barn had already partially caved

in, the stables completely in flames and nothing overhead except the burning skeleton of the roof. The smoke was a red-lit, living thing, swirling with currents caused by the flames. It was hellishly thick and brought instant agony to already tortured eyes and lungs.

Rafe picked his way through the rubble of burning debris cluttering the hall, heading for the far end near the training ring where Warlock was stabled. He heard a beam collapse to his right with a grinding roar and felt the added heat it caused. He couldn't see even a foot in front of him, and nearly ran full force into a stumbling, smoke-blinded Maggie leading a blindfolded black stallion.

Another beam crashed to the ground just behind the horse as Rafe grabbed Maggie and swiftly enclosed her within his rapidly drying blanket. He swore in hoarse gasps when he felt the coughs racking her slender body.

"Get her out of here!" Burke shouted. "I'll bring the horse." He had to yank the lead rope from Maggie's fierce grip, but the trembling horse followed him as obediently as he'd followed the woman.

They were barely out into the sunlight when there was an ungodly roar behind them, and the entire roof caved in.

Maggie didn't know how much time had passed before she became aware of a masklike something over her face and felt the blessed relief of pure oxygen filling her aching lungs. She realized vaguely that the firemen had arrived, too late for the barn but not too late to offer aid.

Breathing happily, she heard voices.

"The next time you start to slug me, brother, I'll knock you flat on your pride."

That, she decided thoughtfully, was Burke. Then she heard York's voice.

"I don't know, Burke. I'll bet Old Shamus himself never looked half so wild when he was fighting Apaches. Rafe might have knocked all your 'science' right down your throat."

"No way," Burke responded firmly.

Then she heard Rafe's voice, more hoarse than normal but cheerful for all of that.

"I'll plead temporary insanity—and can we please drop it? I didn't hit anybody, after all."

"You nearly hit the fireman when he took her away from you," Burke said in a musing voice. "York had to sit on you."

"He did not!" Rafe said indignantly. "He just shoved me and I tripped!"

Maggie, listening to this somewhat puzzling dialogue, suddenly remembered something and sat up with a cry of fear. She pushed the mask off her face, finding herself the focus of a great deal of attention. There were people sprawled all around her on the ground suffering from smoke inhalation, burns, and exhaustion, while firemen moved about and around the still-burning barn.

"Warlock?" she gasped.

"Oh, he's fine." Rafe was staring at her, something she'd never seen before in his eyes. Something dangerous. "You, however, are in imminent danger of being strangled."

Rather hastily reclaiming her mask, Maggie breathed methodically and stared at him over the plastic rim. It would be safer, she decided, to remain a pathetic victim of the fire a while longer.

Except that Rafe obviously wasn't buying it.

"Just as soon as I recover from this godawful morning," he told her politely, ignoring the interested eavesdroppers all around them, "you and I are going to have a long talk, Maggie."

"That should be interesting," York murmured.

Rafe gave him a look. "You aren't invited."

Maggie felt giggles overtaking her, and tried desperately to restrain them. There was nothing, of course, funny about the aftermath of a cruel fire. It was just that the three overpowering Delaney men were gazing at her and their faces were all grimed with smoke and York looked peculiar with one sleeve of his khaki shirt ripped away and a bandage around his upper arm and all of them seemed in a ridiculously comical mood or maybe it was *her* mood that was ridiculous. . . .

Trying to think of something else, she pulled the mask aside to direct a question at Rafe. "Did anyone report the—"

"I think we should all go get cleaned up," he interrupted her briskly, getting to his feet. He lifted a superior brow at York as that brother rose as well. "And since Shamrock boasts several bathrooms, no one will have to stand in line or draw straws for the shower."

"I hate a braggart, don't you?" York asked the eldest brother.

"Insufferable," Burke agreed solemnly.

Maggie was still wondering where she'd lost track of the conversation when Rafe bent down and calmly picked her up. She handed the oxygen mask to a fireman who was fighting a grin, then stared at Rafe. "I can walk," she told him, feeling honor-bound to protest.

"I doubt that."

She didn't really absorb his comment, being too

busy in frowning over his shoulder. "Someone should clean up the mess," she said, outraged by the smoldering clutter behind him.

All three men turned to stare at the ruin of barn four. Then they looked at each other. Then they looked at Maggie.

"Well," she murmured, feeling that her comment had been somehow inappropriate.

Rafe sighed and started up the lane toward the house, carrying his burden with no appearance of strain. "I have never," he said, directing the comment to both his brothers impartially, "seen her quite like this."

"She's a trainer?" York asked, clearly skeptical.

"Best one in the world! She's got Diablo eating out of her hand."

Burke spoke up then, his voice hovering somewhere between astonishment and anger. "You let this poor bewildered child get near your devil-horse?"

"She more or less dared me to," Rafe explained apologetically.

"Oh, *that's* how it was!" Burke seemed satisfied.

"Naturally you couldn't ignore that," York agreed.

Maggie wanted to tell them to stop talking about her, but all her attention was focused on Rafe's right earlobe. She imagined a golden earring and considered the vision thoughtfully. "Gold, but very fine," she said suddenly. "Not bulky."

Rafe didn't miss a step or even blink. "Certainly not bulky," he said, utterly calm.

She directed her owlish gaze to his face. "It'd spoil the effect if it was bulky," she insisted, sensing disagreement. "More pirate than gypsy."

A choking sound drew an offended frown from

her, but both York and Burke seemed perfectly serious. Burke was even nodding slowly with an air of gravity.

"I should think," he said somewhat unevenly, "that very fine and not bulky gold would be perfect."

She smiled blindingly at him, pleased to have her opinion applauded. Then she tightened her arms around Rafe's neck and said simply, "Rafe, I want to go to bed."

Rafe's stony face cracked a bit, and he threw her a laughing glance. "Please, lass. That demand fairly cries out for a less . . . uh, *public* moment."

"But I want to go to bed now," she said solemnly.

"Doesn't beat around the bush, does she?" York murmured.

"She's not herself," Rafe said, adding with a sigh, "More's the pity."

Burke and York exchanged glances, and the elder said dryly, "We won't touch that remark."

"Thank you," Rafe said.

Maggie rested her head on his shoulder, suddenly so sleepy, she couldn't hold her eyes open. "Rafe . . . ? Will you please take me to bed?"

She never heard his answer.

For a second time Rafe carried a sleeping Maggie to her bed. As before, he paused for a few minutes to stare down at her, to push her tangled, smoke-darkened hair away from her face. She looked as if she'd been fighting the devil in his own hell, he thought. Her face and hands were filthy with soot and dirt, and her clothes blackened. He knew she would have felt better after a long bath, but he had no intention of either waking her from the exhausted sleep—or bathing her himself.

He didn't have that kind of willpower.

Nor, he knew, was he in his most patient frame of mind at the moment. Her comical hysteria had sparked laughter that had drained away his rage, but Rafe knew it would be a frozen day in hell before he forgot the image of her dashing into that burning inferno. He felt he'd aged a good ten years in a single morning, and wouldn't be surprised if a glance in the mirror showed him his hair had turned pure white.

Gazing down at her sooty face, he sighed roughly. He wanted to hold her tightly, because he'd come so close to losing her forever. Straightening, he turned and headed for his own bedroom and the shower, his jaw aching from being clenched with determination.

He was going to marry that woman.

After showering, shaving, and changing clothes, Rafe felt a bit more calm and relaxed. He had a word with Mrs. Taylor, the temporary housekeeper, then went into the den to wait for his brothers to finish cleaning up. Glancing at the clock, he was mildly surprised that it was still early morning, but shrugged and headed for the bar in the corner of the room.

Early it was, certainly, but Rafe decided they'd all earned a drink or two. He was on his second when Burke came into the room, and he lifted a questioning brow at his brother.

Burke nodded, then accepted the glass Rafe handed him with murmured thanks. He watched Rafe drain his own glass and immediately fill it, and said mildly, "Not even your hard head can take much of that with your stomach empty."

"Mrs. Taylor's fixing us something," Rafe said in an absent tone. Then he looked at his brother and frowned. "You could have borrowed some of my stuff," he said, noting that although Burke had washed, he was still wearing his smoke-blackened clothing.

"No need. And no need for food for me. I have to be getting back."

"You'll eat before you leave," Rafe said firmly. "Heaven knows I owe you a hell of a lot more than that. Especially for going into that burning barn with me after my—"

"Your lass," Burke murmured, with the same soft brogue that their father had used when speaking the same endearment to his wife.

Rafe looked at him for a moment, then smiled crookedly. "Gave myself away, huh?"

"I believe I got the point when you started to slug me," Burke said. "When you nearly decked that poor fireman, I was reasonably sure."

Rafe dropped his gaze to study intently the glass in his hand, then looked up again when Burke briskly changed the subject.

"I'll file the insurance claim this afternoon."

"No, I'll do that." Rafe shook his head slightly and sent his brother an oblique glance. "You've enough on your mind right now."

"I haven't said so, have I?"

Rafe smiled slowly. "Funny thing about problems. When you have one yourself, it's always easy to recognize the same sort of problem in someone else."

"Some . . . mergers take longer than others, that's all," Burke said.

Rafe started to comment on that, but decided not to. Instead, he brought up something that was worrying him far more because it involved his brother's personal safety. "That crazy bastard out there . . ." He shook his head, feeling a chill as he thought of how close the gunman had come to achieving his goal—and how close he'd come to killing at least one Delaney. "What're you going to do about him? And what can I do to help?"

"I'm going to let Cougar loose," Burke replied with a faint smile. "Take off all the restraints. He'll get the job done."

Thinking of his brother's security chief, Rafe didn't doubt it. He nodded. "Keep me posted, will you? Daily reports, at least. And in the meantime I'd feel better if you flew my helicopter back to Killara instead of your own. Yours should be thoroughly checked out first, and my mechanic's on vacation."

Burke had obviously considered what worried Rafe, because he instantly shook his head. "That bastard's had no access to the copters. He couldn't have sabotaged mine."

"Just the way he couldn't get to you?" Rafe asked evenly.

"I'll handle it, Rafe."

He swore softly. "Right," he muttered.

Burke's tone softened. "Stop blaming yourself. Your security system's set up to protect the stock and buildings, not to protect people. You couldn't have known he'd take a shot at me here."

"I should have canceled the alarms alerting you and York," Rafe insisted. "There was no need to roust you both at the crack of dawn. My people could have handled the fire alone."

"Thanks," Burke said dryly.

Rafe quickly looked up. "You know I didn't mean—"

Burke grinned. "I know. And *you* know that the possibility of something like today's fire prompted us to install that warning system in the first place."

"Those Delaneys," Rafe murmured with a smile that held affection for both his brothers. "One yells help, and they all come running."

"Would you have it any other way?"

"Hell, no."

"Neither would I."

"Nor I," York said from the doorway, and walked into the room. He, too, had cleaned up and, like Burke, was wearing the clothes he'd arrived at the ranch in. "If the bar's still open, I could use a drink."

After searching his brother's face quickly, Rafe handed him one. He wished he could have taken the bullet that had gotten York, but knew better than to say it. His protective feelings toward his brother were deeply ingrained, but York no longer needed protection. "How's the arm?"

"Painful," York said succinctly.

"Put it in a sling," Rafe said. "It'll add romance to your classic profile."

"I already owe you two," York said dangerously. "Don't compound the felony, brother."

Rafe grinned, knowing very well how much his brother hated any reference to his startling good looks. But then he sobered and enlisted York's aid on a topic they both agreed on. "I told Burke he should take my bird back to Killara instead of his own."

"I agree," York said instantly, turning to stare at Burke. "Better yet, I'll fly him in mine."

"I don't," Burke said flatly, "need a guardian."

"Seems to me that's just what you need," York said.

Burke began to pace restlessly around the room. "I'll be fine, I tell you. At the moment I'm more concerned with what Rafe's lost. Although the horses are safe, and the insurance—"

"Won't pay a penny," Rafe said calmly. His mind was a bit sluggish after the various shocks of the morning, but was waking up now.

Both his brothers stared at him for a full minute before realization dawned on them. Burke swore softly while York grimaced.

"No publicity," the middle brother said. "We agreed."

"Which means the fire has to look accidental," Rafe said. "The fire marshall accepted my assurance that the fire was accidental—but the insurance company won't, Burke. If I file a claim, they'll send an inspector out to check what's left of barn four. And he won't have to be a genius to realize that only sabotage could have caused the whole security and fire system to fail."

He shrugged. "So I can't file a claim. If I did, the whole thing would go public."

"Maybe they wouldn't send an inspector," York said, but without certainty. He knew they would, and Rafe's explanation confirmed it.

"They went over my alarm system thoroughly before issuing the policy, and they know damned well it's almost foolproof. *And* the company that installed it was recommended by them in the first place. Since the system failed, they'll want to know why."

"If you file a claim," Burke said heavily.

Rafe shrugged again. "So I won't. The ranch is in the black; I can afford to rebuild the barn."

Burke instantly shook his head. "The funds will come out of corporate profits. The ranch won't suffer just because a madman was trying to get to me." He held up a hand when Rafe would have protested.

Knowing his brother, Rafe finally gestured in defeat. "All right."

"I'll transfer the funds immediately."

"No hurry." Rafe had just realized that without most of her equipment and tack Maggie would be unable to work as hard as she had recently, at least until replacements could be purchased. The thought pleased him, and the gleam in his eyes wasn't lost on either of his brothers.

They exchanged looks, but Rafe was speaking again, intent once more on Burke's safety. "If you won't take my bird, or let York fly you back—"

"I won't."

"Burke—"

Mrs. Taylor came to the door. "Mr. Delaney?" All three men looked at her, and she seemed a bit uncertain. "I've prepared a meal—"

"Thank you, Mrs. Taylor," Rafe said, gesturing for his brothers to precede him. He followed, marshaling arguments against Burke's stubbornness.

He was still protesting when he saw both his brothers off some time later; he was resigned by that time to losing, but he was clearly unhappy about it. He and York both checked Burke's helicopter in spite of his objections, but neither was at ease even after the checks showed no tampering.

"Call when you get home," Rafe said, holding Burke's gaze with his own.

Burke laughed softly. "Yes, Papa."

"And be *careful*," York added fiercely before turning toward his own helicopter.

Rafe called after him, "And *you* have a real doctor take a look at that arm!"

A wave was his acknowledgment, and Rafe stood back as both helicopters lifted from the pad moments later. He watched them head in their different directions, then grinned when, as he'd expected, York's bird turned and began trailing Burke's. Rafe had a feeling Burke would probably see or sense his escort, and would no doubt curse York heartily over the radio. But York would follow him safely home to Killara nonetheless.

And none of them would have had it any other way.

When Maggie woke, the dimness of her bedroom told her it was late afternoon. Her throat hurt, aching dryly, and she felt stiff and sore. She sat up and swung her legs off the bed, yawning, realizing only then that she'd slept in her clothes. And what clothes! Dirty, grimy, reeking of smoke—

Smoke?

In a split second it all came back to her. All of it. The fire, the horrifying race to save the horses, an insane sniper's gunfire . . . and her meetings and subsequent conversations with the Delaney brothers.

Maggie wished that God had taken those memories and locked them away where she would never have found them.

Staggering a bit, Maggie walked into her bathroom and peered into the mirror above the vanity—and groaned. Dear Lord. Not only had she sounded like a madwoman, she looked like one!

Her hair was tangled, filthy, and smelled of smoke—like the rest of her. Her clothing was torn and impossibly dirty, her hands blackened, and her face was streaked with soot. If Rafe had looked a casualty of a war after his infamous brawl, she looked like a casualty of *three* wars.

And obviously her side had lost.

She dived for the shower, swearing continuously. She was not a vain woman, but the thought of what Rafe's brothers had seen—and heard—absolutely horrified her. And she couldn't help but wonder if Rafe himself had undergone a change of heart after seeing her at her worst. She wouldn't blame him if he had.

It was one thing, she thought wryly, to state one's intention of marrying an Irish brat with nothing but a love of horses to commend her, but quite another to maintain that certainty in the face of a soot-blackened woman who'd lost her wits under pressure.

Nearly scrubbing her skin off in the process, she managed to remove all the grime and smoky odor from her body and hair, and the steam from the hot shower eased the dry ache of her throat. Clean clothing felt wonderful, and her hair dryer helped the glossy highlights to reemerge in her golden hair.

Then, squaring her shoulders, Maggie left her room to brave the lion. Or, in her case, the gypsy. Had she really babbled something about a gold earring?

Mrs. Taylor almost literally pounced on her the moment she entered the kitchen, and Maggie found herself very meekly eating a sandwich and silently revising her initial impression of the woman. Obviously the housekeeper had decided that Maggie needed looking after, and she seemed to enjoy scolding the younger woman for her dash into the burning barn. It was equally obvious that the story had gotten around.

Maggie's uneasy question about the where-abouts of the Delaney brothers produced an answer that relieved her somewhat. Rafe was down in the compound, Mrs. Taylor reported, and the other two had gone.

So she had only one to face, Maggie thought. Only! If the rage she recalled seeing in his eyes had been real and not her imagination, one Delaney was probably more than she'd be able to cope with anyway.

She felt even more certain of that when she reached the burned ruin of barn four and found a frowning Rafe surveying the damage. The barn was still smoldering in places, but there were no firemen. A few Shamrock employees were poking around in the debris in search of anything salvageable.

Maggie stood well back for a minute and watched Rafe's face. She jumped slightly when Tom's quiet voice spoke at her side.

"A crew's coming tomorrow to rebuild."

She looked at the foreman, puzzled. "Here, you mean? But won't the insurance company need to inspect what's left and discover what caused it?"

"Sabotage caused it," Tom said calmly. "That's why Rafe interrupted you when you started to ask if the sniper had been reported. That was what you were going to ask, wasn't it?"

"Yes. You mean, it hasn't been reported? The police haven't been informed?"

Tom smiled a little. "No. And they won't be. The Delaneys will take care of the problem."

"Alone?" she exclaimed.

He chuckled. "Those three together . . . they'd

storm hell with no more than a bucket of water between 'em. For that matter, each one'd storm the pit alone. Burke, he'd figure to wheel and deal, and the devil'd find himself done out of his pitchfork and brimstone. York would fight like ten men and leave the place in a shambles."

"And Rafe?" she asked softly.

"Rafe . . ." Tom shook his head and smiled. "He'd fight like ten men too. Then offer to buy the devil a drink after it was all over."

Maggie turned her gaze back to Rafe. No, the Delaneys weren't royalty, she thought, but they were kingly men. Strong, sure men. Though each could fight trouble alone, they banded together to meet it, finding an extra measure of strength in that unity. It was a kind of closeness that brought a lump to her throat and made hot tears dam behind her eyes.

"How—how did the other two know there was a fire?" she managed to ask.

"They have an alarm system rigged up between them," Tom explained. "When our fire alarm went off, it was followed five minutes later by alarms in Killara, Delaney Tower in Tucson, and Hell's Bluff. If ours had been a false alarm, Rafe could have canceled the other three. Works the same way at the mining town, the offices, and the homestead. Any breach of security or problem that triggers the alarm anywhere alerts all three of the brothers."

"They seem very close."

Tom nodded. "They are. I doubt anything could come between them. But that doesn't mean their . . . magic circle couldn't open up to include others. That'd just make the circle stronger." And with that cryptic comment, Tom strolled away.

Maggie stared after him for a moment, then

jumped a second time when another voice—this one hoarse and slightly unsteady—reached her.

"I want to talk to you!"

Guardedly she watched Rafe approach. Working on the theory that it was best to spike guns whenever possible, she didn't give him a chance to start in on her. "I'm sorry," she said somewhat breathlessly as he reached her.

Hands on hips, he stared down at her. "For what?" It wasn't an incredulous question, but rather one strongly implying there was an entire list of sins, and which one was she apologizing for?

Linking her fingers together in front of her, Maggie was barely able to meet his dangerous eyes. "Well, for everything. Sorry the barn burned. Sorry I was rude and—and hysterical with your brothers. Sorry you had to go into the barn after me. . . ."

"That all?" he asked curtly.

Well, Maggie *was* sincerely sorry for all those things. But she'd be hanged, she thought rebelliously, if she'd apologize for anything else! "That's all."

Rafe drew in a deep breath, and his voice emerged in its modified lion's roar. "You could have been killed, you little idiot! Just what in hell did you mean by running back into that barn?"

Maggie's hands found her own hips and her shoulders stiffened. Her temper was definitely rising, and she forgot the danger in his eyes. "You know damned well I went in after Warlock!" she answered in a roar of her own. "What's more, I'd do it again! And don't you criticize me for that, you arrogant—"

Surprisingly Rafe began to laugh. His black eyes were gleaming down at her, and the crooked, endearing smile curved his lips. "Had me worried for a minute there, lass," he said cheerfully. "The way you were apologizing and wringing your hands, I thought I'd broken your spirit!"

She stared at him, bemused.

He caught her suddenly in his arms, holding her tightly. "You scared the hell out of me with that stunt," he said thickly. "Don't you know I'd lose every horse in creation before I'd give you up?"

"Even one worth his weight in gold?" she whispered.

"Even that one." He drew back slightly, looking down at her with eyes brimming with tears. "If we'd lost Warlock, it would have broken my heart, lass. If I'd lost you, there wouldn't have been a heart to break. Or a life worth living. I love you, Maggie."

She felt her own heart turn as she realized something she had not allowed herself to see before now. This man, this kingly man with the pride of a prideful family at his back, this strong and charming man with the devil in his eyes—was also a vulnerable man. Because he loved and admitted to loving, with no assurance that his love was returned.

"I . . . don't want my ranch anymore," she told him unsteadily. "And I don't want your ranch. I just want you."

He went very still. "Why?" he breathed.

"Because . . . I love you. Oh, Rafe, I love you so much!"

His shaking hands lifted to frame her face. "I hope you mean that, lass," he whispered. "I'll not let you take it back now."

"I mean it. Rafe . . ."

He kissed her tenderly, fiercely, lifting her up

into his arms to hold her in a strong and loving embrace. "It's about time!" he told her hoarsely.

And Maggie wasn't even embarrassed to hear a cheer as he carried her up the lane toward the house, or to see the people of Shamrock watching with smiling faces.

She was just glad the kingdom approved their king's choice.

Nine

"Just leave dinner in the oven, would you please, Mrs. Taylor?"

Maggie didn't lift her head from Rafe's shoulder until the kitchen door swung shut behind them, and then her only comment was a mild "You don't care how much you embarrass me, do you?"

Rafe was carrying her steadily toward his bedroom. "My love," he said huskily, "the entire ranch knows by now that I finally won my lady. Why not Mrs. Taylor as well?"

"It's your insufferable Delaney pride, that's what it is," she told him glumly. "You just *have* to advertise my downfall."

"I thought I was advertising mine," he murmured.

Maggie made a rude noise, but she was smiling, and her gaze was fixed lovingly on his face. Curiously she felt no nervousness or shyness, no uncertainty or fear. Her inner certainty was, she realized, an affirmation of the love she felt for Rafe, and her last doubt had faded to nothing.

Blinking suddenly, she saw that they'd reached the doorway to his bedroom. And he had stopped. Meeting the black eyes gazing at her quizzically, she smiled. "Second thoughts?"

"Never. Are you going to marry me?"

She felt a laugh forming somewhere deep inside her, in that warm part of her he had brought to life. Gravely she asked, "Is my answer a prerequisite to crossing that threshold?"

"Yes."

"If I said no, you'd put me down?"

His jaw tightened and black fire flashed in his eyes, but he replied steadily. "I'd put you down."

"You mean"— she began toying with a lock of his hair and absently nudged her shoes off—"that even though I love you, even though I'm very much afraid I couldn't live without you and wouldn't say a word in protest if you wanted no strings at all, even now, when I'd do just about anything you asked, you still want a ring and a promise?"

"Even now," he said huskily. "Especially now. I love you, Maggie. Will you marry me?"

"Just as soon as you can find a preacher," she said.

His entire face seemed to light up at her words, and the breath caught in her throat at the fierce tenderness in his eyes. He kissed her swiftly, carrying her into his bedroom and kicking the door shut behind them. Maggie saw little of his room; she had eyes only for Rafe. But she did notice the king-size bed.

He set her on her feet beside it, and a shaft of late-afternoon sunlight slanted through the window to turn her golden hair into a halo. He cupped her face in warm hands, looking down at her as if he were looking into heaven.

His head bent, and his lips feathered kisses along her jaw and down her neck. One hand tangled in her hair while the other slowly unfastened the buttons of her blouse one by one. Maggie found her own arms around his waist, her hands tugging his shirt from the waistband of his pants.

She had to drop her arms to allow her blouse to fall free, but her hands returned instantly to the buttons of his shirt. While he shrugged free of the garment, she explored the muscled strength of his chest, her fingers threading among the springy dark hairs to find the firm flesh beneath. An unfamiliar liquid heat swirled to life somewhere within her body, and her heart seemed to be shaking her with its pounding.

She gasped softly, her hands finding his shoulders and gripping fiercely, as he trailed kisses past the shadowed valley between her breasts, over the lacy bra, and down the quivering flesh of her stomach. He unfastened her jeans, and the heavy material slid roughly against her skin as it fell to the floor. She kicked the jeans aside as he rose, her arms lifting to circle his neck, pressing her body against his with a sudden fierce need composed of too many sleepless nights and a love too long denied.

Rafe groaned, his lips finding hers hotly in a kiss that left her trembling. If his arms hadn't been locked around her she wouldn't have been able to stand upright. She clung to him, unable to breathe and not worried about it, giving him her heart and soul in a single blinding instant.

In feverish haste he rid her of what little clothing

remained, then his garments fell to lie on the floor with hers. He bent to strip the covers back, then lifted her and placed her on the wide bed. He joined her immediately and every caress slowed to a tender and savoring touch, as if he had mastered time and bent it to his will. He gave them all the time in the world, and filled every second with loving her. He touched her as if she were something infinitely precious—and something he was starving for.

The slight abrasiveness of his work-roughened hands brought her flesh to shivering awareness, and Maggie barely heard the kittenlike sound of pleasure emerge from her throat when eager lips captured the hardened tip of one breast. She wove her fingers through his hair, her body moving of its own volition to press even nearer to him. She was on fire, burning with a spiraling tension winding tighter and tighter, urging her toward something she could only sense without understanding.

The hungry pull of his mouth and the gentle, erotic probing of his fingers fed the fire until it was a living, molten thing in her veins. She couldn't be still, couldn't breathe, couldn't hold back the soft moans rising in her throat. Her hands roamed over his strong back, kneading muscles, tracing the length of his spine. And her body moved instinctively to cradle his when he rose above her, the breath rasping harshly in his throat.

Maggie heard throaty, shaken pleas coming from some lost and frantic place inside her, heard his husky murmurs in response, and she cried out wildly when he joined her completely, the sudden shock a curiously primitive, compelling expansion of her desire. Fiercely she held him with muscles unknown until then, her body rocking with his in a sensuous dance.

Tension, aching and restless, built steadily, coiling like a live wire until it had to snap, shattering her every nerve with a pleasure that was very nearly unbearable. . . .

Rafe couldn't seem to stop touching her, his hands gliding over her flesh gently, compulsively. Maggie found no fault with that. She cuddled even closer to him, dimly aware of the day's last sunlight making a valiant effort to brighten the room. She wanted only to remain near him, touching him, feeling his arms around her and his heart beating steadily beneath her cheek.

She felt secure as never before, at peace and at home in his arms, and when she drifted off to sleep, it was with the trusting suddenness of a child.

She woke once in the night, the moonlit room showing her an urgent, rekindled fire in black eyes, and went into his arms eagerly, naturally, proving that she could tame a devil-man as thoroughly as she could tame a devil-horse.

Maggie felt the sunlight first, hot across her eyes, and turned her head fretfully to escape it. The action wakened her even though she didn't open her eyes, and she tried to figure out what was bothering her. Sunlight, she thought muzzily. *Morning* sunlight. But there had been afternoon sunlight as well, hadn't there? Her room didn't boast two exposures.

Rafe's did.

Her eyes snapped open, and she found herself staring up into his. He was raised on an elbow beside her, a morning beard darkening his jaw and his thick black hair tousled, smiling very tenderly.

"Uh . . . hello," she said a bit uncertainly.

His smile deepened. "Hello," he responded politely.

"What time is it?" She didn't really care, but felt honor-bound to ask. Besides, she had to say something, and since she had absolutely no experience in carrying on a conversation in a man's bed . . .

"It's around eight, I think." He smoothed a strand of golden hair away from her face, his hand lingering to trace the line of her jaw.

For some reason Maggie didn't bother to probe, the touch of his hand robbed her of shyness. She smiled at him and lifted her own hand to push back the lock of hair falling over his forehead—something she'd wanted to do more than once these last weeks. Then his words sank in. "Around *eight*? Lord, I haven't slept past six o'clock in years."

"Yesterday," he reminded her, "was a very busy day, love. Which is one reason we're both going to take today off." He reflected for a moment while she stared at him. "As a matter of fact, we may take a week off."

"But the horses. The work . . ." It was a weak protest, and Maggie was astonished at herself. She hadn't taken—or wanted to take—a vacation since she was sixteen.

He leaned over to kiss her, gently at first. "I think," he said huskily, "that there are enough people on Shamrock to take care of the horses for a few days." His lips toyed with hers while flaming black eyes gazed into hers. "And I think you and I . . . have earned some time alone together, love."

She felt the strength flowing out of her, replaced by quivering awareness and surging need. Her arms slipped around his neck as she felt his weight pressing her back into the bed, and for the first time in years she happily pushed work out of her mind. . . .

Even though Maggie had known Rafe to be a demonstrative man, she was nonetheless unprepared for just how loving he could be with all restraints gone. Feeling in love and loved, Rafe was tender, passionate, affectionate, cheerful, humorous. He touched her and watched her almost constantly. And he glowed. His eyes, his smile, his entire face glowed with happiness.

That might have been too much for some women, might have been a burden, because it was scary to see oneself as so vitally important to another human being's happiness. Maggie felt humbled by that realization, but it was no burden. For the first time in her life she knew herself to be loved and trusted to a degree she'd never dared hope for, and that certainty gave her the freedom to love equally in return.

As the days passed Rafe and Maggie were inseparable. They didn't go down to the compound until after the weekend, and might not have gone then had Maggie not insisted that everyone on Shamrock probably thought them dead by now. Rafe had protested having to put his boots on, but Maggie had dragged him outside to observe the work on the new barn. And both had been touched by the fact that every employee of the ranch found time to congratulate them wholeheartedly on their obvious love.

In the house they spent time as lovers do, just being together. They slept late, shared meals and showers, opinions and lifetimes. And secrets.

Maggie discovered one secret quite by accident one day as she was searching through Rafe's closet for a blouse. (Mrs. Taylor had her own way of showing approval of the relationship: She had begun putting away all their clothing in his bedroom.) Rafe was shaving in the bathroom, singing cheerfully, and Maggie smiled to herself as she listened. He was quite definitely addicted, she thought, to that song about Irish eyes.

As she reached for her blouse, one of her feet dislodged a large box lying on the floor of the closet. She shrugged into the blouse before kneeling to straighten the box. But a very familiar scent wafted up to her from the box, and she hesitated. She buttoned her blouse, then gave in to curiosity and lifted the lid of the box.

When Rafe came into the bedroom a few minutes later, he found Maggie standing, hands on hips, staring at him.

"What've I done?" he asked, instantly assuming the mien of a beaten spaniel.

"You," she said lovingly, "should be locked up. It's not safe for you to run around loose. I imagine your brothers have paid a bundle to keep you out of an asylum—which is where you belong."

Rafe was innocently hurt. "Really, love, that's not a very nice thing to say. What, by the way, makes you think I'm crazy?"

She stepped to one side and gestured. On the bed behind her lay an outfit. A rather curious outfit. It was buckskin, with lots of fringe. and a very colorful Indian headdress lay beside it.

"You had me fooled," she told the miscreant dispassionately. "I thought it was you from the first, but that cinnamon scent made me doubt my other senses." She picked up a small pouch, tied with a drawstring, and waved it at Rafe like an indictment. "But this is how you fooled me. Cinnamon in a pouch! The scent was so strong that I associated it with a stranger." Staring at him, she tried to keep her mind off the raw virility of his strong body clothed only in a towel.

"Can I defend myself?" he asked.

"I don't see how," she said, letting her temper show. "Not only did you play a sneaky trick on me, but you got the whole ranch in on it! That perfectly *lovely* story about the Shamrock kissing bandit showing up here every spring! Rafe, you—"

He stepped forward and caught her in his arms.

Minutes later she said a bit weakly, "That's not fair, dammit."

He was kissing her neck. "Mmm . . . but I had to hold you, lass, and you'd hardly let me near you then."

Maggie made a gallant attempt to gather her scattered wits. "I wouldn't let you near me? I couldn't *stop* you, you conniving—" Long moments later she added a defeated "Oh, hell," and abandoned the world.

The cinnamon pouch was somewhat crushed, and the whole room smelled of it, but neither of them minded.

They spent one day in what Rafe called the Journal Room—that room Maggie had found in the old part of the house containing his collection of steins and the maps and journals of the Delaney family. He showed her several particular journals, including Old Shamus's—which proved to be a frank and cheerful account of a strong man in rough times, a man with an incredibly deep sense of family and a powerful will.

"He really did say it!" Maggie said. She was reclining on the pillows they'd stolen from the den, and looked up from the yellowed pages to grin at Rafe. "He said he'd build a dynasty!"

Rafe chuckled softly. "He didn't lack for conceit, did he?"

"I don't think you could call it conceit. He did it, after all." She glanced at the journal Rafe was thumbing through. "Whose was that?"

"Falcon Delaney." He shook his head. "He was—no pun intended—a strange bird. Very well educated for his time, and a bit mysterious. Spent some years as a Texas Ranger."

Intrigued, she asked, "Mysterious how?"

Rafe held the leather book up and gestured with it. "Well, it's obvious he left out more than he recorded in this journal. There are some cryptic references to important men of that time, and some of the entries are in code."

"You've never tried to have it deciphered?"

He smiled disarmingly. "No one else bothered and I could never bring myself to have it done. I suppose I was always afraid the decoded entries would be very commonplace and unexciting. As long as the code isn't cracked, I can let my imagination roam."

Maggie looked at his strong, unconventional face, the wonderfully expressive black eyes, and felt her heart turn over with love for him. "Do you know how much I love you?" she asked solemnly.

"Tell me," he murmured, reaching for her.

Merlin showed up for the first time in days, a bit thin and seemingly preoccupied. He wanted only food and a brief snooze in Rafe's chair before disappearing again.

"We should have kept him in," Maggie told Rafe, anxious. "He looks like he could use a few square meals. Doesn't he realize this is home?"

"Of course, he does, lass." Rafe pulled her comfortably into the circle of his arms where they sat together on the couch. "But you know how it is. Tomcats in the spring . . ."

She smiled and linked her fingers together behind his neck. "I haven't noticed you wandering," she said.

"That's because I have everything I need right here." He kissed her tenderly. "An Irish lass who holds my heart."

Her smile widened at the soft cadence of his deep voice. "Do you realize how Irish you've gotten yourself? More and more with every day that passes. No brogue, but your voice has the rhythm."

"Does it bother you?"

"Bother me?" She laughed softly. "Darling, I love it!"

"I love you," he whispered, and she forgot about tomcats.

On Friday morning a special messenger arrived at the house while Maggie was in the den, carefully cleaning a very old Spanish saddle that was another piece of the Delaney history Rafe kept preserved. Rafe came into the room, sat down on the couch, and dropped a large manila envelope in her lap.

Sitting cross-legged on the floor, she had been industriously polishing a silver buckle, but put aside the cloth and buckle to pick up the envelope. "What's this?" she asked.

Rafe sat back and smiled at her, but his eyes were grave. Apparently ignoring her question, he said musingly, "I think you still have a . . . tiny reservation about us, love. True?"

She gazed at him for a long moment, then took a deep breath and nodded, unable to destroy the trust between them by lying. "It isn't anything I can put into words," she explained seriously, getting up to sit beside him on the couch, still holding the envelope. "It's just a feeling that I'm . . . inadequate somehow. I mean, well, you *know* where you came from. You know what bloodlines combined to make you what you are. You know your own history. And I don't know mine." She gestured slightly when he would have interrupted. "Oh, I know it doesn't matter to you what my background was. And it doesn't really matter to me—except that I wish I could *know*."

She laughed a little shakily. "It isn't a reservation, Rafe. It isn't a doubt, isn't uncertainty. And it isn't about *us*. It's about me. I know who I am and where I am. I'd just like to know where I came from."

He tapped a finger on the thick envelope in her lap. "Then open this, lass, and you'll see where you came from."

"What?"

He smiled at her confusion. "I knew you felt . . . uncertain about your background, your family's history, and I knew it bothered you. So, a while back I called Cougar Jones, who handles security for Delaney Enterprises. He's a handy man to know, and I've never yet seen a question or request stump him. So I told him I needed a genealogy traced. He knew of someone back East who does that kind of thing, and here it is."

She looked down at the envelope, then lifted glowing eyes to his. "You did that for me?"

He leaned over to kiss her gently, then gave her a stern look. "There's one thing though. As you said, your background doesn't matter to me. So no matter how many horse thieves you find on your family tree, lass, you're still going to marry me! Understood?"

She nodded meekly. "Understood." She wasn't entirely certain she wanted to know her bloodlines now that the answers were right in her lap, but she opened the envelope anyway, because she had to know.

Whoever had assembled the material, she saw immediately, had done a thorough job. Not only was there a detailed family tree going back several generations, but there were also biographical summaries of the principal O'Rileys. The spelling of the name had changed more than once—just as the Delaney name had been altered, Rafe confided. Both bent their heads over the papers.

"Would you look at that?" Maggie said in amusement. "I'm Irish both sides practically back to the apple!"

Rafe started laughing suddenly and pointed to a name. "You see that? I happen to know that name."

"Don't tell me . . . ?"

"That's right. He was a horse thief. A rather

famous one too." He grinned at her. "I told you we made a terrific team. I'm descended from a cattle rustler, and you're descended from a horse thief!"

"Well," she said dryly, "if we lose all our stock, we'll both know one way of getting more, won't we?"

He suddenly pulled her into his arms, crushing a sheaf of papers between them. "Do you know," he said huskily, "that's the first time you've said *we*?"

"I like the sound of it," she murmured, smiling at him.

"I love the sound of it." He sat back and reached into his pocket, pulling out a small black velvet box. "It's what I've been waiting for."

She stared at the box, then her eyes widened when he flicked the catch with his thumb to reveal a ring nestled inside. It was obviously a very old ring, the golden shank finely made and warm with the smooth glow of age and care. It was set with a beautiful opal surrounded by diamonds. The opal was alive with glints of pink and green fire, and the diamonds shone brilliantly.

"Not a traditional engagement stone," Rafe said softly, watching her face. "But a special ring. The Spanish don brought the stone up from Central America, and had the ring custom made for his Delaney bride. I took it to a jeweler to have it cleaned. The opal's your birthstone, isn't it, Maggie?"

She looked at him and nodded, her heart too full for words.

"I think it'll fit. Her hands were tiny too." He took the ring from its box and slid it onto the ring finger of her left hand. It fit perfectly.

"Rafe . . ." Her voice was hoarse, but her eyes said what her throat wouldn't allow.

He pulled her back into the warmth of his embrace, neither of them noticing when the genealogy papers fell to the floor.

"I have to fly into Tucson tomorrow morning," Rafe told Maggie much later that night. "A board meeting. Why don't you come along? You could see something of the city."

Cuddling closer to his side, she yawned sleepily. "No, you'll be busy. Besides, I really need to make at least one appearance down in the compound and *try* to get some work done."

"If you insist."

"I do." She was nearly asleep when a worry surfaced. "Rafe? Your brothers'll be at this meeting?"

"Of course."

Uneasily she said, "You came back from Hell's Bluff looking as though you'd fought a war, and both your brothers left here after fighting a fire. What's going to happen in Tucson?"

"A stuffy board meeting," he assured her. "Burke will tell us a lot of things we won't understand, and York and I will be bored stiff. That's why they call them board meetings, you know."

She ignored the attempt at humor. "But somebody shot at Burke while he was here, and hit York and—" She took a deep breath. "Just . . . be careful, will you, please? I think you and your brothers should build a concrete bunker for your little get-togethers."

Rafe chuckled softly. "We'll be fine. The Tower has excellent security, and Cougar'll watch over us all."

Maggie wasn't completely reassured, but when Rafe was dressed the next morning, she forgot worry in the enjoyment of his appearance. "You look," she told him from the depths of the bed, "like the devil in an angel suit."

Having abandoned any feelings of guilt over lounging in bed past dawn, she hadn't argued when he'd told her to stay put. Now, gazing at him as he adjusted the knot of his tie in front of the dresser mirror, she couldn't help but giggle.

"Thanks a lot," he said.

He was dressed from neck to foot in solid white. Three-piece suit, shirt, tie, shoes—all were white. And while another man might have looked most peculiar in the outfit, it fit Rafe perfectly. It set off his dark good looks and his cheerful mood. He had taken attire meant to be formal, she realized, and made it into something else. Jaunty. Rakish. Devilish.

Knowing the man she loved, she cocked a questioning brow. "Rebelling?" she asked politely.

He turned to grin at her. "Something like that. Burke likes us to be businesslike at these blasted meetings. I borrowed a pair of coveralls from one of the maintenance men once and showed up like that. I thought he was going to deck me."

She giggled again. "Well, you'll certainly startle them today."

He walked over to the bed, then leaned down, his hands on either side of her, and kissed her. "I'll let you know what the reaction is. By the way, I have a present for you."

"You do?"

He straightened and smiled at her. "I do. It's in a box, and here in the house. Somewhere. It's up to you to find it."

It took Maggie only a moment to understand his motive, and her voice caught him just before he left the room. "Rafe! You're just saying that to keep me from working. I'll search this house and not find a thing."

"If you search the house, you'll find it," he said. "And I know you'll search, lass. You've too much Irish blood not to be curious." He winked.

Maggie threw a pillow at him, but he was already gone.

Two hours later, she found it. Swearing but amused, she climbed up on a chair and wrested the box down from the top shelf of Rafe's stein collection. It was a dress box and, opened, revealed a dress. An absolutely beautiful dress fashioned of lovely violet silk. She knew without looking at the size that it would fit. It was long, with full sleeves and a deep V neckline. A pair of matching high heels, wrapped carefully, were also in the box.

She had no earthly idea when or where he'd gotten it, and wondered at his reasons even as she pulled the dress from its box and admired it. That was when she saw the note. It was short and to the point, the handwriting as bold as the man and his demand.

> *Pack a few things, lass—including this dress. We'll leave when I get back.*

Now, where, she wondered, were they going? Someplace she'd need a formal dress, obviously. And then, unbidden, she remembered Rafe saying that the brothers still dressed for a meal at their mother's table. At Killara.

Killara?

Maggie badly wanted to see the place where Rafe had grown up, see the homestead that Old Shamus had defended so successfully from Apache raids and Mexican bandits and whatever else had come along. She wanted to see where the Delaney family had founded their dynasty. She really did want to see that.

She *didn't* want to see Burke Delaney.

Wincing, she remembered her behavior during and after the fire. How in the world was she going to be able to meet Burke's amused green eyes? She wasn't ready for that, she knew. She'd never be ready for that.

But she packed. She knew her Rafe.

It was late that afternoon when she heard him in the kitchen, cheerfully telling Mrs. Taylor that he and Maggie would be gone for a day or two. When he came into the den, she had only a moment to note the discarded coat and tie, and the shirt sleeves rolled up to reveal his bronze forearms. Then she was pulled up from her chair and hugged fiercely.

"I missed you, love."

She looked up at him and saw signs of strain that would have been invisible to anyone else. "Rafe, what happened in Tucson?"

He smiled, one hand lifting to brush a strand of hair from her face. "In the end . . . a tempest in a teapot," he said. "But a violent storm while it lasted." He wasn't smiling any longer, and his black eyes were somber. "I hadn't realized before how some things are beyond our control. How we're all vulnerable to loss through . . . outside influences. It wasn't me on the rack this time. But it could have been me."

"Your brothers?" she asked softly.

"Burke." He shook his head. "I'll tell you about it

later. The only thing I want to tell you now is that I love you, Maggie. So very much."

She gazed up into eyes that were once again smiling tenderly. Hugging him, she murmured, "I love you too." After all that, it was a little difficult to air her grievances. But Maggie tried. "Rafe, you aren't taking me to Killara, are you?"

"Of course, I am. Are you packed?"

"Yes, but—"

"Good, then we can get started."

"But, Rafe—"

"Where's your case?"

"There, by the door. Rafe—"

"Come along, love."

Maggie dug in her heels. "Rafe! After the way I acted during the fire, I don't want to see either of your brothers! Talk about lousy first impressions."

He smiled down at her. "My love, my brothers are shortly to become your brothers-in-law. Now, I enjoy visiting both brothers whenever time permits, and occasionally they come here. Do you propose to hide in a closet, or what?"

She groaned. "I just don't think I'm ready—"

"Hey." He cupped her cheek in one warm hand. "Apart from your own feisty personality—which is very endearing, in case you didn't know—you also boast the sterling quality of making me deliriously happy. First impression and all, my brothers will love you like a sister. And besides all that . . ." His smile went a bit crooked, vulnerable. "I need to go home, lass. I need to look at Killara. Okay?"

She smiled tremulously, warmed by the trust he showed in allowing her to see his vulnerability. "Okay. But if both your brothers try to talk you out of marrying me, don't say I didn't warn you."

He laughed and led her through the house, barely

giving her time to wave to Mrs. Taylor as they passed through the kitchen. At the helipad he stowed her case in back, explaining that he always kept clothes at Killara for himself. Then he buckled her into the passenger seat and went around to his own side. Moments later they were lifting from the ground.

There was little conversation within the helicopter while it headed east. Maggie was happy despite the coming meeting with at least one of the other Delaney brothers, content to gaze at Rafe's strong profile and watch his hands moving expertly at the controls of the aircraft. She returned his frequent smiles, feeling truly at peace for the first time in years.

Watching him, she saw his eyes narrow suddenly, and followed his gaze to see another helicopter approaching from the east. A Delaney helicopter, she realized. Burke's? Before she could ask, the other craft had passed them, and she barely made out two figures within it, one of whom gestured at Rafe. A thumbs-up gesture. Rafe spoke quickly into his headset, then apparently listened to the response.

Then he was laughing. "Well, well," he said cheerfully. "It looks like the clan's all here. That was Deuce—a friend of York's—in that bird. York's at Killara."

"You mean, I have to face *both* of them?" She groaned.

He grinned at her. "Don't jump out. You haven't got a parachute!"

Maggie grumbled to herself, but when they lifted over a mountain range moments later, she forgot to be worried.

It was spread out below and before them,

painted in glowing reds and oranges by the setting sun, nestled in its valley with a sprawling air of belonging. It was a feeling, Maggie realized, of time and battles, and much love, a feeling of family and unity.

"Killara," she murmured.

Rafe smiled at her, love and tenderness alight in his eyes. "Killara," he said, and headed the helicopter for home.

THE EDITOR'S CORNER

Home for the Holidays! Certainly home is the nicest place to be in this upcoming season . . . and coming home, finding a home, perfecting one are key elements in each of our LOVESWEPTs next month.

First, in Peggy Webb's delightful **SCAMP OF SALTILLO,** LOVESWEPT #170, the heroine is setting up a new home in a small Mississippi town. Kate Midland is a witty, lovely, committed woman whose determination to save a magnolia tree imperiled by a construction crew brings her into face-to-face confrontation with Saltillo's mayor, Ben Adams. What a confrontation! What a mayor! Ben is self-confident, sensual, funny, generous . . . and perfect for Kate. But it takes a wacky mayoral race—including goats, bicycles, and kisses behind the bandstand—to bring these two fabulous people together. A romance with real heart and humor!

It is their homes—adjacent apartments—that bring together the heroine and hero in **FINNEGAN'S HIDEAWAY,** LOVESWEPT #171, by talented Sara Orwig. Lucy Reardon isn't really accident prone, but try to convince Finn Mundy of that. From the moment he spots the delectable-looking Lucy, her long, long shapely legs in black net stockings, he is falling . . . for her, with her, even

(continued)

off a ladder on top of her! But what are a few bruises, a minor broken arm compared to the enchantment and understanding Lucy offers? When Finn's brothers—and even his mother—show up on the doorstep, the scene is set for some even wilder misunderstandings and mishaps as Finn valiantly tries to handle that mob, his growing love for Lucy, law school exams, and his failing men's clothing business. A real charmer of a love story!

In the vivid, richly emotional **INHERITED,** LOVE-SWEPT #172, by gifted Marianne Shock, home is the source of a great deal of the conflict between heroine Tricia Riley and hero Chase Colby. Tricia's father hires Texas cowboy Chase to run Tricia's Virginia cattle ranch. Their attraction is instantaneous, explosive . . . as powerful as their apprehensions about sharing the running of the ranch. He brings her the gift of physical affection, for she was a child who lost her mother early in life and had never known her father's embrace or sweet words. She gives Chase the gift of emotional freedom and, at last, he can confide feelings he's never shared. But before these two ardent, needy people can come together both must deal with their troublesome pasts. A love story you'll cherish!

In **EMERALD FIRE,** LOVESWEPT #173, that marvelous storyteller Nancy Holder gives us a delightful couple in Stacy Livingston and Keith

(continued)

Mactavish . . . a man and a woman who seem worlds apart but couldn't be more alike at heart. And how does "home" play a part here? For both Stacy and Keith home means roots—his are in the exotic land of Hawaii, where ancestors and ancient gods are part of everyday life. Stacy has never felt she had any real roots, and has tried to find them in her work toward a degree as a marine biologist. Keith opens his arms and his home to her, sharing his large and loving family, his perceptions of sensual beauty and the real romance of life. You'll relish this exciting and provocative romance!

Home for the Holidays . . . in every heartwarming LOVESWEPT romance next month. Enjoy. And have a wonderful Thanksgiving celebration in your home!

Warm wishes,

Carolyn Nichols

Carolyn Nichols
  Editor
LOVESWEPT
Bantam Books, Inc.
666 Fifth Avenue
New York, NY 10103

His love for her is madness.
Her love for him is sin.

Sunshine and **Shadow**

by Sharon and Tom Curtis

COULD THEIR EXPLOSIVE LOVE BRIDGE THE CHASM BETWEEN TWO IMPOSSIBLY DIFFERENT WORLDS?

He thought there were no surprises left in the world ... but the sudden appearance of young Amish widow Susan Peachey was astonishing—and just the shock cynical Alan Wilde needed. She was a woman from another time, innocent, yet wise in ways he scarcely understood.

Irresistibly, Susan and Alan were drawn together to explore their wildly exotic differences. And soon they would discover something far greater—a rich emotional bond that transcended both of their worlds and linked them heart-to-heart ... until their need for each other became so overwhelming that there was no turning back. But would Susan have to sacrifice all she cherished for the uncertain joy of their forbidden love?

"Look for full details on how to win an authentic Amish quilt displaying the traditional 'Sunshine and Shadow' pattern in copies of SUNSHINE AND SHADOW or on displays at participating stores. No purchase necessary. Void where prohibited by law. Sweepstakes ends December 15, 1986."

Look for SUNSHINE AND SHADOW in your bookstore or use this coupon for ordering: